Marriage, She Wrote

Unsuitable Suitors

Book Two

Ebony Oaten

Snow Goat
Publishing

ebook ISBN: 978-1-923735-05-7

print ISBN: 978-1-923735-06-4

Marriage, She Wrote

Spirited Demeter Mellingham rushes into making poor decisions. She finds herself exiled far from temptation in north Wales, after dropping her entire family into a pit of scandal.

She nurses a broken heart, certain her gallant Captain Tenby will return to rescue her from the relentless rain and crushing isolation. But as weeks turn to months with no word, doubt begins to creep in, as insidious as the Welsh damp.

When two exotic springbucks arrive as gifts from the Prince Regent, Demeter is given a chance to prove her newfound maturity. Alas, the male of the pair immediately leaps a six-foot hedge and disappears into the countryside. Now, Demeter is not only disgraced, she is on the verge of humiliating her family in front of royalty, who she expects to arrive any day now.

Lloyd Alwyn, the estate's handsome and frustratingly competent overseer is everything Demeter's captain is not: grounded, practical, and undeniably present.

Lloyd has always thought too thoroughly about problems, and has missed out on love before. Is he about to miss his chance with the enchanting Demeter Mellingham?

Prologue

February 1816
February 16
Bangor Hall

Dearest Mama,

This is a dreadful state of affairs. I did no wrong. I was on my way to wed the gallant Captain Tenby. The Captain said the anvil was mere hours away when our axle broke. That's not my fault. You cannot blame me for something that was completely out of my control. The weather has been dreadful across the entire country, apparently. As an aside, I cannot wait for summer, so we can see an end to this hideous gloom.

I repeat my point, none of this is my fault. Falling in love is completely natural. You said so yourself. Why has Papa sent me so far away? Why not simply bring me home where I can explain all? I now find myself in the middle of nowhere. This is most unfair.

The moment Captain Tenby and I are together again, we shall wed, you will see. Then all will be well.

Your darling Demeter

March 2,

    Penrose House,

    Bath

    Dear Demeter,

I have only today received your letter and hope this does not take as long to reach you as your missive took to reach me. The fact of the matter is you remain unwed. Eloping is enough of a scandal, but failing to elope has brought unspeakable shame on us all. The fact is, no matter your intentions, your carriage never made it to Gretna Green. Your 'wonderful captain' has not returned.

We have also heard rumors that he may not be all he claims.

Can you truly not appreciate how much your actions have brought the whole family low? Especially your sisters, whose very seasons in London are at risk! I am also punished in that I must remain in Bath under the appearances of taking the waters for my nerves. I am even further in my brother's debt as his wife has agreed to chaperone Persephone and Hestia for their season. We can only hope that people do not make the connection between my brother and his wayward niece. You must remain where you are, until things can smooth over. Pray your sisters make exemplary matches and in due time all can be well again.

    Your loving mother.

March 20,

    Bangor Hall

    Dearest Mama,

The mail is incredibly slow. I am beside myself, for Captain Tenby has made no contact and I fear for his health. I am hoping that the moment I send this to you, I shall receive word from him and all my

panic will be for nothing. If he does not, it must indicate he is in a terrible situation. Why else would he not to be able to send a message of any kind after such a long time?

It should be a lovely spring day here, but it's raining and miserable. If I cannot return to London, at least let me hasten to Bath, where I shall be with you again and amongst some proper company. There is absolutely nothing to do here. The Marquess and his wife are trying their best to be accommodating, but their newly wedded bliss is making them unsuitable for company. I believe Amelia is involved in reading business letters!

Yes, business letters!

You think I'm a disgrace? The lady of the house is conducting trade. Even the Dowager is involved! Clearly this is not a fit place for me to be in residence. If you are concerned for our family's reputation, you should send for me immediately, so that I am not tainted by association.

I shall make haste to Bath at your first word.

In my heart, I know Captain Tenby is completely honorable. Once he knows where I am, he will come and claim me and we shall be wed. Then all will be well.

Your darling Demeter.

April 10,

Bangor Hall,

Dearest Mama,

I pray your most recent letter is on its way to me, but I could not wait another day longer. I am ruminating into complete mold. I have more cobwebs than a scarecrow and I am wearing the same clothes day after day! Partly because there are no events to attend, but mostly because I have only one warm dress to keep me comfortable in this inclemency.

Will the rain never stop? There is so little to do here, I have even taken up walking along the Menai. It is a lovely river. The tides are

dramatic and distracting – somewhat. There, I have found one good thing to report. That does not, however, cancel out all the many dull things here. I am not ashamed to admit I am so lonely here, I have taken to talking with the Lord's overseer and we discuss crop rotations!

Let me come home, or at the very least, let me come to Bath!

Your darling Demeter.

Ps, The Marchioness and I are friends. She is a rather lovely and jovial person, despite dealing in trade. I was correct, she is still heavily engaged in business. Even worse, I have found the business a rather pleasant distraction. Are you completely mortified by my utter fall from grace? Then send word and I shall be at your side.

April 20,

Bangor Hall

Dearest Mama,

I can only assume your most recent letter to me was waylaid. The weather here is ghastly. That's not merely my opinion alone. The families here are saying it's unusually cold and wet. I'm sure it's much more pleasant in Bath. Tell me all about Persephone and Hestia's seasons. I cannot obtain any information about London society all the way out here. I have taken to reading the news sheets but they are filled with reports of crops and sale prices, and of course the awful weather. At least I have things to discuss with the overseer.

Please let me come to Bath. Please?

D-

April 25,

Bangor Hall

Dearest Mama,

I know you have not had a chance to reply, but I miss you so much. I

even miss Persephone and Hestia. It rains every day here. I have
attached a cutting from the newssheet describing how bad the weather is.
It's all anyone can talk about, so it's not just me complaining of the
damp.

D-

May 10
Bath
My dutiful daughter,
*I have forbidden your mother to write any more
missives to you. I have also withheld your last two
letters from her sight. Your earlier correspondence has
caused her terrible distress. The weather in Bath is just
as awful as it is in north Wales. Did you think it was
only raining in Bangor? To specifically punish you?*

*I beg you to be sensible to your situation, and the
strain you have placed the entire family into because of
your failed elopement, and how it reflects on your
Mama and myself as parents of such a willful and
disobedient child.*

*It has now been several months and your captain
is nowhere to be found. What will arrive first, Christ-
mastide or your Captain?*

*At least you are not in London to ruin your
sisters' seasons. They have borne up magnificently
under the pressure of scandal and catty gossip. Despite
their dowries and your aunt and uncle's best efforts,
they have yet to find a suitable match. I am now*

indebted to them.

Speaking of dowries, it pains me to report that Captain Tenby has not made contact to ask for yours; another reason to believe he has no intention to wed you.

You shall remain exactly where you are until you can prove you have developed a sense of responsibility for your damaging actions.

To this point, your new charges will arrive soon. They are a gift from the Prince Regent. As you claim to be in dire need of distraction, this will do well for you. Look after them and keep them safe and out of trouble. They must be in excellent condition for the Prince's visit. Do not disturb your mother further, she is at her wits' end.

Yours etc.,

Chapter One
May 29, 1816

Bangor Hall
North Wales

Her father's letter burned worry into Demeter Mellingham's heart as she headed down the stairs to breakfast. She stopped by the tall windows of Bangor Hall to read it again in the watery morning light. There it was, written in her father's own hand – the prince regent would be visiting!

How would they get Bangor Hall ready in time for such an esteemed guest? More importantly, would it stop raining by then?

Even more importantly, when was the prince planning on arriving?

Shaking her head with concern, her attention wandered to the nearby flowing waters of The Menai Strait. This morning the banks were high. Water lapped the hedgerow at the bottom garden. The green lawn had developed brown patches as the grass drowned in the wet, salty water. The foreman was out there, checking the water levels or whatever it was he did for the Rosstrevors. From the grin on his face, his chance of ending up even more drenched than usual seemed to delight him.

At that moment, he turned and saw Demeter standing on her dry side of the glass. A flinch of discovery caught her and she had to pretend she was looking at the river, not he. The man touched his cap in greeting and sent her a smile that cut through the gloom.

The rogue.

It wasn't Demeter's fault the foreman reminded her of Captain Tenby. He had curly dark hair that was often wet from the rain, and a strong brow with slightly wild eyebrows. From this distance, she wondered if his eyes were the same light brown as her gallant captain's.

Toasted bread aromas wafted up the stairs. Time to get to the breakfast room. The bright yellow curtains in here fought a losing battle with the grey skies on the other side of the window panes. Demeter made a swift curtsey to all and proceeded to fill her plate with toast and butter, then she checked the table for the dish of marmalade.

Excellent, there was plenty left.

Her mind snagged on some of the words in her father's letter. Two new charges? That concerned her even more than the prince's visit. They would be arriving soon, according to his letter, and they would need to be in … what had her father written? 'excellent condition' for the visit. What an odd way to speak about people.

Poor lambs, being sent away from the palace! What apparently dreadful thing had they done to irritate the prince?

Lack of sunlight was making so many people melancholy. Perhaps there was not much sun in London either? Father has said the weather was just as bad in Bath, so it was possible the capital could be shrouded in wet as well. Maybe that was why Prince George was sending people away – he was in bad humors from the poor weather.

Whoever they were, they would need to get used to the early mornings here. Demeter was doing her best, but she was always last to arrive for breakfast. These days, she arrived early enough to greet the Rosstrevors before they went about their duties. She was glad to have arisen early this morning, because she needed to speak with them.

As she took her seat, Demeter knew the entire household would be whirling faster than 'The Swellies' which appeared without warning in the Menai waters, once she shared the news.

She put her bundle of letters down and retrieved the most recent epistle to make sure she was reading it correctly.

"Salutations of the morning, my lord, my lady. I don't mean to throw the house into disarray, but my father sends word that the prince regent will be visiting."

Time stood still. The Marquess froze in place, a fork of food half-way to his mouth. His mother's mouth fell open, then she closed it with a snap. His wife's brows rose high and stayed there.

Eventually, David Rosstrevor put his fork down and spoke. "The Prince Regent? Is coming here?"

"That's what it says in my father's letter," Demeter confirmed, folding the paper to the pertinent part, and passing it to him so that he may read it for himself.

He immediately handed it to Lady Rosstrevor, who said something like, "Does it, now?"

The Dowager rose from her seat and moved to her ladyships' shoulder, her mouth turning down at the edges as she also read the words.

Amelia Rosstrevor read the letter out loud, "New charges arrive soon … They must be in excellent condition for the Prince's visit." Oh goodness, there it is. Then he goes on to say, "Do not disturb your mother further, she is -"

"- That part isn't important." Demeter interrupted, hoping to retrieve the paper and spare any comments about the rest of its contents. Then the Rosstrevors would truly know how disappointed the Mellinghams were about what she'd done. They knew to some extent, of course, as her father had written and asked them to take her in, all those months ago.

Amelia Rosstrevor's brows dropped into a crease. She nodded her head as she counted the weeks dates in her head. "We don't know when, but I do hope it does not occur during my confinement."

The dowager spoke. "It is an honor to receive such a visit, but it would have been prudent to check with us first." She turned to her son and said, "Are you sure the prince did not write you?"

David Rosstrevor paled somewhat and cleared his throat. "I have seen no such correspondence. Are we sure the prince means to visit us *here*? Perhaps your father means he'll be in the general vicinity. How odd that he should know before we do?"

"I will write my father for further details," Demeter said. "I agree, it's difficult to ascertain. My first thought was that the Prince was coming here, to Bangor Hall. Also, my father says the prince is sending me two charges to take care of. Why are people referred to as 'charges' instead of 'people', and why would he not check with your good selves before sending more guests here? Has he sent an earlier letter directly to you asking about this?"

Lady Rosstrevor turned to her husband and said, "We've had nothing directly from your father since you arrived. We did find one yesterday, which was for you. It must be the one you are showing us now. We did write to him at the time of your arrival to let him know you were safe and well. He replied with a brief note to say that he was satisfied with the news. Then we heard nothing." The lady absently rubbed her palm over her belly. "This is the first correspondence we've seen from him since then. I am relieved you saw fit to show it to us, but also, I am discombobulated as to its contents."

The Dowager Marchioness shook her head and made her way back to her seat. "It's most vexing. Until now I would not have thought the prince cared much about us. He's not trying to reclaim Caernarfonshire is he?" She refilled her teacup and asked nobody in particular, "Perhaps he is planning a procession of some kind? The cathedral is lovely. I'm looking forward to seeing my grandchild baptized there. I shall write to Dean Warren and ask if he has any information."

David Rosstrevor shook his head and turned to Demeter. "It's as well that you brought this to our attention. Please write to your father for more information about when the prince will arrive and what his needs may be. While you're at it, ask him for the name of a secretary or courtier who is organizing the visit. It's a strange thing that we should be hearing about this most important news via your father, and not from someone within the palace itself."

Demeter read the letter again and could not for the life of her work out what her father meant. Why would the Prince of Wales be visiting such an out-of-the way place?

If only her mother had been the author of the letter! The very first line would have focused on the Prince's visit. The rest of the letter would have been dense with detail, not added as an afterthought at the end of a thorough dressing-down about her failure to wed.

Chapter Two

Demeter finished writing her letter to Papa and gave the paper to Lord Rosstrevor. There was room for him to add anything further, should he so want to. Instead of taking up a quill, he handed it straight to his wife and muttered something about inspecting their stock of sealing wax.

Checking the window, she noticed the rain had finally stopped. No time to lose, she'd get some fresh air before the next downpour trapped her indoors again.

Not that she'd ever admit it, but a walk along the ever-changing waters of the Menai Strait did much to restore her equilibrium. The perambulations gave her time to think, or time to *not think at all*, which was also a lovely way to spend time.

She had so much time, after all.

When she did think, it was of her darling, Captain Tenby, and when he might return. He had not asked for her dowry because … because he was so honorable, of course! They weren't married, yet.

It hurt her soul not to have word directly from Mama, especially as she hoped her mother would relent and invite her to Bath.

But no, her father kept them apart.

She could curse his name with every drop that fell from the heavens. And there were so many drops falling relentlessly!

The other detail that truly hurt, all the way to the depths of her soul, was the salient fact that her beloved captain had not returned. Nor had he found a way to make any contact at all. It had been months!

They had been so in love. Such an emotional, giddy and exciting time in her life.

Now her head filled with doubts and her thoughts swirled like the Menai waters.

How had her father known Captain Tenby hadn't contacted her? Oh, of course! Father had read her letters to Mama. As head of the family, he had that right. If she were married to Captain Tenby, Papa would no longer be in charge of her, nor would he be reading her correspondence.

If only that stupid axle hadn't broken!

Such shockingly bad luck.

They *were* in love. Her parents simply hadn't understood – and still didn't seem to understand. The captain loved her. He was a hero from the continent. Not that she knew exactly what he'd done - that wasn't something women discussed, because they didn't need to know the details of war.

It was all such a terrible misunderstanding, her heart said. It warred with her common sense, which nagged at her and demanded her attention. Why had Tenby not made contact?

Angst and frustration took hold. Tenby *should* have written by now.

Were the Rosstrevors withholding his letters? From her encounter at breakfast it appeared to be Lady Rosstrevor who read the arriving correspondence and dispersed them to their intended readers. His Lordship didn't seem fussed about reading much at all.

The letter from her father had been unread when she'd

received it. The wax had snapped cleanly and the folds were crisp. No sign of a steamed entry.

The way the family had reacted to the news of the prince's visit also appeared genuine. If they'd read her mail first, they would have been organizing the house before she'd awoken.

It didn't seem to make any sense. If the Rosstrevors weren't interfering with her mail, and she had not heard from Tenby, perhaps he had not written to her after all?

She stepped in a puddle. Drat!

The pathway down to the jetty, where several boats huddled together, was slippery and full of muddy puddles. At this time of year, there should be wildflowers growing in the meadows. Not much was blooming, in the wet. The daffodils that Wales was famous for had barely made an appearance this year. Not even the ever-reliable cotoneasters were putting out much. Back home – oh it had been so long ago – the gardeners at their summer estate used to complain bitterly about those particular plants. Cotoneasters made lovely hedgerows with their small green leaves and sprays of red berries. Alas, they had the habit of vigorously growing wherever the birds deposited the berry seeds. In the potato beds, in other hedgerows, even in the driveway. Left unchecked, they quickly became unmanageable.

At the jetty, Demeter saw the foreman again. He nodded another greeting to her, and she returned it. What a convenient excuse to get closer to him and see if his eyes were the same color as her beloved's.

They were a deep nutty brown, much to her surprise. This close to him, she chided herself for thinking he was anything like her captain. This man was a little taller and somewhat leaner. His wild eyebrows suited him, giving him a commanding appearance.

The foreman delivered another smile, and heaven help her, she couldn't help feeling a glow of warmth coming her way. How starved of company must she be to entertain such emotions?

He excused himself from the conversation he was having with

the boatmen and turned her way. "Miss Mellingham, are you hoping to visit the island today?"

Should she? The water in the strait ran in such changeable directions, a safe crossing was never guaranteed. How might she cross in such a small boat?

She found herself asking, "How long do you think the rain might hold off?" instead, as she didn't want to appear afraid of a little water.

The boatmen chuckled, they must have overheard her question.

As if in answer, a few drops fell and the water's surface soon splattered. Ripples spread in widening circles.

The foreman shrugged and looked up to the skies. Dark ribbons filled the heavens, indicating fresh bands of rain heading their way. "There goes any chance of an excursion," he said. "I'd best be getting you back to the big house. Word is a pair of animals are arriving soon, specifically for you."

Demeter stopped for a moment. "You know about them?"

"Yes, they're a fine pair. Only got word this morning. That's why I was down by the river getting some extra help on the off-chance we might need it." He replied, and indicated she should walk on ahead of him. "Very flighty creatures, so I'm told."

A laugh burst forth as realization hit her. "There I was thinking my new charges were people, but I do believe you are speaking of livestock."

"Of course, I am. I doubt they'll think much of our rain where they're from either."

Confusion piled on confusion. Demeter would be in charge of animals, not humans. That … made a lot more sense, now that she thought about it. But what kind of animals?

"What are they and where are they from?" Demeter asked.

With a chuckle, the man said, "That would be telling. There's so little that happens around here, a surprise is well worth the wait."

As they reached the driveway to Bangor Hall, an enormous, closed-in wagon arrived. Excitement at last! Her heart thrummed at the possibilities. Could her new charge be a pony? That would brighten her dreary life! The foreman bid her farewell and ran toward the wagon to direct the human and animal traffic.

As she came closer, the wagon looked so much larger than her first impression. Perhaps this new charge was more than a pony. A real charger - a horse that only she could ride, but whom nobody else could touch. Yes, the very thing! A sleek chestnut stallion who brooked no other but her, with her kind hands and gentle touch. It would have a glowing coat the same color as the foreman's eyes.

She shook her head, wondering where on earth that thought had come from. Picking up her pace, she ran to where people were gathering.

There seemed to be a great deal of shouting. The foreman, whose name she still didn't know, was directing people yet remaining composed in the sea of excitement.

As she neared the wagon, she ripped a tuft of grass and held it in her palm for the stallion to eat; their first act of trust.

It was an enormous surprise to Demeter that the animal which ended up looking her way was not a glossy stallion at all, but a small, horned antelope.

It had a fawn-colored back, mostly white body shaped like a barrel and dramatic dark brown stripes along its sides.

It took a tentative step toward her on the spindliest legs she'd ever seen. Its nostrils sniffed the air near her outstretched hand.

Demeter had never seen anything like it. It could be a deer, but its horns were far too long and ... they spiraled to sharp points behind, a little like a goat's.

She made a quick note to herself to never approach it from the rear, otherwise she risked being impaled.

The animal's body was completely out of proportion to anything she'd seen before. Its torso was rounded, covered in what she hoped was soft fur. Would it let her pat it? But its legs were so thin! Below the knee, it couldn't possibly hold the deer's - or whatever-it-was's - body upright.

"What's it called?" Demeter asked out loud, to nobody in particular.

One of the workers shouted, "She's called Elizabeth."

That had people chuckling.

"Very funny, but what is she?" Demeter called out, then she said to the beast, "Hello Elizabeth. It's lovely to meet you. Have some grass."

The foreman said, "It's a springbuck."

A spring buck. She'd never heard of such a beast. Could this be an animal from Asia somewhere? Perhaps it was an exotic species from Australia. She'd been reading about them some time ago. Their proportions defied belief!

But this creature was very much real, and standing in front of her.

Its large ears and small nose flickered with the unfamiliar sounds and smells on the wind. The little creature's entire body shivered for a moment. Poor thing, must be freezing.

It might not be the wild stallion she'd imagined, but it sure was a wild animal. Everyone else seemed scared of it, but the timid creature sniffed the air and took a tentative step closer to Demeter. As if by sheer force of will, Demeter held her hand out steadily, determined not to shake. Her shoulder ached with the need to remain steady. Her palm may as well be holding a heavy sack of flour as a few blades of grass, such was the effort.

The wind swirled and changed direction. The little antelope's nose twitched at the new scents.

"Everything is fine, little one," Demeter said, as if the beastie could understand her. Perhaps if she spoke to it in ... gosh, what language would it be used to hearing?

The animal suddenly skittered sharply right and ran off at incredible speed.

Stunned, Demeter stood there a second, then shook her head

and gave chase. The rest of the men quickly overtook her, but even they were not fast enough!

The foreman nearby made magnificent strides, but he was no match. Did the creature have a hidden set of wings?

Demeter stopped running and panted for breath. "Come back!" She shouted.

The animal's spindly legs sure were strong. In a matter of seconds, it was well clear of those in pursuit.

Demeter cried, "She's getting away!"

The workers slowed down and gave up the chase one by one. There simply was no point in trying anymore, the spring buck was already too far away, and far too fast.

The creature was wild, and weird, and had such lovely brown eyes with the most incredible lashes. And an elegant neck she had not had time to appreciate.

The foreman shook his head as he returned to Demeter. He retrieved his hat, which had blown off in the chase, and flicked the raindrops away before putting it back on his head. "I suppose when you're used to being chased by leopards and such you develop a good sprint. The poor thing must be terrified in this cold, wet place."

"Leopards chase the spring bucks?" Demeter had heard of leopards. "Does that mean she's from Africa?"

"Indeed. From the Cape Colony."

"Goodness, she is a long way from home. The poor thing must miss its family terribly," Demeter said, thinking of how much she missed her own.

Instead of melancholy nostalgia, Demeter then began to feel the first icy pinches of fear. This was supposed to be her animal to care for on behalf of the prince regent. To prove she was responsible and reliable and ... oh all of that stuff her father cared about.

The one the prince would come and check on.

But what really hurt Demeter the most was her pride. The

creature had not trusted her over all others, as she'd hoped. It had not eaten from her palm; had not become her pet.

The foreman sighed and said, "Don't worry yourself, Miss. There's a six-foot hedgerow keeping him in, and the big gates at the front. He'll not get far."

A couple of the workers were still in pursuit, but by this stage it was a more leisurely amble than direct chase as exhaustion claimed them. The hedge loomed ahead. The springbuck must soon realize she was fenced in.

Demeter urged the foreman, "Call your men away, Mister … I don't yet know your name, I apologize."

"It's Alwyn."

"Mister Allen, I don't want them to scare her. She'll be fine once she gets to know the area. I don't want her to die of fright."

The foreman nodded to Demeter and shouted to his men, "Leave it be, we don't want to run him ragged." Then he turned to Demeter, a curled lock of damp hair falling over his forehead, "Lloyd *Alwyn*, at your service."

"Oh, I am sorry, I misheard over the commotion. Mister Alwyn."

The men near the animal mustn't have heard his entreaty to cease their pursuit, or they were ignoring him. One of them lunged at the creature.

It darted out of his grasp, and headed for the hedge. The silly thing must be blind with panic. The branches were far too thick, it would not get through the-

It did *not* get through.

Instead, it leapt into the air and cleared the tall hedge with room to spare. In the air, the creature's white underbelly contrasted starkly against the grey sky.

Demeter gasped at the animal's athletic prowess.

Mister Alwyn swore under his breath.

The workers kicked the ground and also swore.

Demeter eventually said, "You were right, he was a he after all."

Mister Alwyn smacked his hat against his thigh in frustration. "I see now why they're called *spring* bucks."

But Demeter did not care about that any more. The creature had sailed out of sight. The animal she was responsible for. How on earth had anyone managed to capture it in the first place if they could leap about like that?

More than that. How in heaven's name was she supposed to explain this calamity to the Prince Regent?

Chapter Three

Not for the first time, Lieutenant Colonel (ret.) Lloyd Alwyn wondered if he would ever be suited to life outside the services. When he'd been in the army, he'd understood the rules. As had everyone else. There was a certain logic to daily life in the service that provided comfort. For example, one would order others to stop running, and they *would* stop running.

Immediately.

Alas, the events of this morning had shown how diametrically opposite un-regimented life could be. Right in front of him, the farm hands and stable boys had paid his directives no heed at all.

In fact, they'd appeared to enjoy the chaos, which only puzzled him more. They had singularly failed to curtail the spring buck, and yet they were now sharing a laugh at their own expense, celebrating their ineptitude.

Did they not under-

He stopped his thoughts. He was about to mentally chastise the men for not understanding how important the spring buck was. Yet, there's no way they could have known this.

In the army, it wouldn't have mattered if you didn't know *why* you were being asked the do something (or cease doing that same something). It only mattered that someone else up the chain had decided. which meant everyone below them followed through.

Such simple rules provided certainty and order. It's what he'd needed after his romantic disappointment. Not that he'd ever admit he'd run away to the army because a woman had rejected him. Perish the thought.

No. Life was simply better with order.

Even when things were chaotic on the battlefield, there was still order.

He turned to the woman who had not dissolved into hysterics, must to his surprise. "Miss Mellingham, before the noisy lads reach us, we should check on the second spring buck."

Her mouth made the most distractingly adorable 'o' before she said, "There is another? In that case, let's do exactly that."

What an agreeable woman, he thought.

Looking in on the second animal, this one was about the same size as the other, but it had narrower, thinner horns.

Miss Mellingham said, "Let's fashion a harness into leading strings."

"Grand idea," he readily agreed. If this animal leapt high like her friend, whoever was holding on to the strings should keep them safely anchored.

Making sure the doe was securely enclosed, they walked together to the stables in search of equipment to use.

Miss Mellingham put her hands to her waist as she looked about. "I don't wish to alarm you, Mister Alwyn, but the Prince Regent is planning a visit, to check on his two charges. I've already lost one, I will not let the next out of my sight."

The Prince Regent?

Here?

Time to focus! He began directing the returning stable hands to find the smallest buckles and thinnest leathers. This time, they did listen to him and sprang into action. In the space of an hour, they had a harness they could affix around the remaining spring buck to stop her bucking off.

Now to get the contraption onto the skittish beast without it leaping into the heavens.

Miss Mellingham held her palms out for the straps. "I think it best if I enter the wagon with the spring buck … or spring doe … and affix the harness."

One of the boys interrupted, his face pale with worry. "Miss, I think one of us should do that. It could injure you."

Miss Mellingham breathed in slowly and rounded her eyes. It reminded Lloyd of the way a cat fluffed itself up to appear bigger.

In a low voice she said, "Considering how you frightened the other one away, I believe I am best placed for this task."

Lloyd had to press his lips together to stop a laugh bursting free. The boys and men in here backed off, showing utmost respect. He wouldn't mind a bit of that respect himself.

As Miss Mellingham made her way to the wagon, he turned to workers and said, "Right lads," it was astonishing how much his 'commander' voice had them paying attention. "We are to receive a distinguished visitor in July. That doesn't give us time to squabble. These stables must be spick and span, not a stick of chaff out of place before then."

The men simply stood there and looked at him.

"Get on with it, then!" He said.

They spun around and headed into the stalls, mucking them out. Well, those stalls would barely stay clean for an hour, let alone another month or so, but at least they were doing something.

The youngest stable boy turned around to him and said, "Who's coming, Mister Alwyn?"

Questioning a command? If this boy had behaved like that on the peninsula, he would have been unceremoniously dismissed.

But they weren't in the army now, and it appeared that people needed a reason to do what they were told.

Fine then.

"None other than the Prince Regent himself, who will be visiting to inspect the progress of the *two* spring bucks delivered here today. Not only do these stables need to be spotless, the prince will notice one of them is missing. The first person to bring the buck home safely will be permitted to meet the prince himself."

Stunned silence followed.

Then men fell about laughing uncontrollably. Their spluttered comments merged together.

"What a jape!"

"Coming here?"

"The Prince Regent!?"

Another voice joined in, it was Miss Mellingham re-entering the stables, with a skittish spring buck in the harness they'd made. "Please keep it down, you'll scare her."

As one, they stopped. The critter's thin legs skittered on the flagstones. Her long ears flicked back and forth. Miss Mellingham held out some soft grass. The doe pulled at a few dainty strands, then chewed vigorously.

Once again, she seemed to have complete command over the others. Where on earth had she learned that?

The men set to clearing the stables once again. Recent history told them the spring buck would not likely be contained by the shoulder-high timber walls. However, once the large barn doors were closed, Lloyd was reasonably confident it would not escape.

Unless the thing could leap through the roof.

One of the boys nudged his elbow into the one next to him and called out, "Oh, Miss? Did you know the Prince Regent was paying us a visit?"

Miss Mellingham secured the Spring doe's harness to a hook on the wall and closed the animal in. Then she turned to them and said, "I did. My father wrote the very thing in his last letter to me. I then informed their lordships of the news. I sent a message back to my father, just this morning, asking for more information. The buck and doe are gifts from His Highness, and he will be arriving personally to inspect their progress."

The color drained from their faces as she relayed this. Again, Lloyd had to press his lips together to keep his laughter at bay. They hadn't believed him when he'd said it only a moment ago. A few stern words from her, and they looked set to faint!

Luckily, they did not faint. Instead, one of the workmen said, "Then I suggest we get this place ... err ..." he looked to Lloyd, "Spic and span. Is that right?"

Lloyd nodded, and found himself smiling at Miss Mellingham's ability to keep these wastrels in line. He could learn so much from her.

If he were being completely honest with himself, he needed to learn from his past mistake as well, and not dilly-dally when it came to romance.

Chapter Four

Another day, another heavy grey sky full of rain. Demeter was in the orchard, realizing it was a silly place to be if she wanted to remain dry. The trees were not protective like the sturdy old oak near the front gate, which provided shelter in sun and rain.

The branches were so laden with water, every movement created an extra shower upon her head.

She inspected the branches, looking for tell-tale blossoms that should be reaching for the sun. Alas, the branches only had leaves; no blossoms and no budding fruit.

The garden staff would know better than she, but she felt sure little apples and pears should be evident by now. They'd best hurry up if they were going to be ready for an autumn harvest.

Taking the cuttings back to the stables, she took extra care opening the small side entry. No sudden moves, obviously. That would scare the horses as much as her young pet. She made sure she didn't open the door too widely either, on the off-chance the creature might be on the loose. The moment she squeezed through, she made sure it was securely closed behind.

The stable hands were here in great number, cleaning and

sorting things out. She wasn't surprised to see so many in here, it was dry and warm in the stables, unlike working in the yards.

The doe stood guard in her pen; ears high, nose twitching. Demeter felt sorry for the lovely creature. "Yes, darling, it is very strange and different."

She held the green leaves forward and the doe sniffed the air. It didn't appear hungry. There was a bundle of fresh dry feed in the wall basket, so it wouldn't starve.

What did these creatures eat, exactly?

A gust of wind preceded a fresh burst of rain landing on the roof. Mister Alwyn was in the stables as well. He stepped up to the stall and said, "You should get to the kitchens and warm up. You won't be able to look after her if you catch a chill."

What a considerate man.

A stable hand stepped up and asked, "Is there anything else you'll be needing, Miss?"

"Yes, I need someone to remain here overnight, just in case she calls to her friend who is out there somewhere." Then for good measure, she added, "The poor beast."

The stable hand accepted her gentle chastisement and said, "Of course, Miss. There are usually a few of us in the gods," he pointed to the mezzanine where bales of straw sat piled in neat stacks. "I'll make sure I'm one of them."

"Thank you," she said, grateful the doe wouldn't be left alone. Even with other horses in here for company, they were enormous in comparison and might frighten the doe. "I wonder if I should have a cot in with her, so I may remain overnight to keep her company?"

"I can stay in there with her all night, Miss, if you need. I'm used to sleeping rough. You should stay in the big house in a proper bed. I won't let anything happen to her. I'll make sure of that."

Mister Alwyn chimed in with a, "Good lad".

The boy lit up the barn with his smile and said, "Everyone calls me 'Roberts'."

Relief filled Demeter at his enthusiàsm to be singled out. Then noisy rumbles erupted from her stomach.

Mister Alwyn asked, "Have you eaten at all today?"

Now that she thought about it, she had not. From the moment she'd woken this morning, she'd thought of nothing but the spring doe and how they were to get the buck to return to her.

Mister Alwyn led her out of the stables. The walk to the kitchen was splashy work. Demeter's feet ached with cold as water seeped through her boot stitching. Mr. Alwyn overtook her and had the kitchen door open by the time she reached it. What a thoughtful man.

The moment they were both inside, he secured the door closed and indicated she should take the closest seat by the ovens. Baking bread aromas sent her spirits soaring. Her stomach created fresh bout of noises. Heat roared up her face in embarrassment at how aggressive they sounded.

Mister Alwyn said, "Fresh bread with a little cheese and relish will soon see you right."

There were a great many jackets and shawls hanging from the pot hooks, cloying the air with humidity. It wasn't what Demeter expected, to see so many items of clothing here. It took her a few minutes to appreciate why the kitchen was doubling as a laundry. With so much rain, clothes on the lines would come back wetter than they'd gone out.

The pots were stacked together in towers on a nearby card table. The thin table legs under all the weight of the cookware reminded her of the spring doe's shape, a big body on stick-thin legs.

It was so lovely and warm in here. Her loose hair curled as she removed the shawl at her neck. When she hung the shawl from the hooks above the oven, drops of water landed on the hotplates with dramatic hisses.

The maid came in and asked if they needed tea. Demeter and Mister Alwyn answered at the same time in the affirmative.

"I shall write my father again," she said to Mister Alwyn. "Now that the doe is safely ensconced in the stables. Perhaps she might call to her friend and he will call back to her, and their ..." she stopped and collected her thoughts. "What noise *does* a spring buck make?"

Mister Alwyn blinked and looked confused for a moment. "I haven't the faintest idea!"

When the maid returned with tea and some vittles, Demeter requested a writing set, so she could update her father on progress. Only yesterday morning she'd given a letter to the Rosstrevors to send along to her father. She would write another today. There was no time to wait for a reply. It could be weeks!

"Dearest Father, the charges have arrived. They are a pair of spring bucks. They are in excellent condition."

There was little point telling him one had escaped already. She hoped to have it back before the prince arrived. Then nobody ever needed to know.

"Please tell me everything you know about their care and feeding. They are from the Cape Colony and must be feeling the cold. The barn here is warm and dry, and well-stocked. The Prince Regent will be delighted to know they are in excellent care. When will he be arriving?"

That should be enough. No point writing a long epistle when it would arrive so soon after her last letter. Knowing her father, he might take his time in drafting a reply, which was bound to be short and lack detail. If only he'd let Mama reply.

CHAPTER FIVE

The doors to the Rosstrevor's study were wide open, so Demeter walked in with a singsong, 'Knock, knock.'

David Rosstrevor, the Marquis of Caernarfonshire, was leaning back in a chair, a broad smile on his face. His new Marchioness and his mother were poring over papers.

All three looked up as Demeter walked in.

The Marquess smiled broadly and asked, "How goes your exotic beastie in the barn?"

"She is well, and has nibbled some of the hay. She does not appear to want to drink, yet. Also, I picked some leaves off the apple trees but she didn't eat any - at least, not while I was looking on. Perhaps she needs privacy to eat?"

The Marquess sighed and asked, "Were there any apples growing on the trees?"

"I didn't see any. I did make sure that the branch I took was barren, though. Mister Alwyn is out now examining the orchard."

Rosstrevor nodded and said, "I'll go and have a look myself right this minute." He then refilled his tea cup.

Perhaps 'right this minute' meant something else in Wales?

Best not get sidetracked, she was here on a mission. "I came to see if there were any letters for me today, my lord and ladies?"

The Marquess looked to the two ladies and raised an eyebrow. The women made sad expressions and shook their heads.

"Are you absolutely sure there is nothing for me? There appear to be rather a lot of letters on the table."

The Marchioness stood up from behind the desk. "I'm sorry we don't have more news. Especially as your father says the Prince Regent will visit. We are waiting with bated breath for the reply to your letter ourselves. As we only sent it yesterday, it could be a fortnight before it reaches Bath. We may not hear back from him until June. We do hand over every letter that arrives for you."

As much as Demeter didn't want to believe it, she accepted the Marchioness at her word. Her lips wobbled with the thought Captain Tenby might never make contact.

As if reading her mind, The Marchioness said, "I can imagine the weather is getting everyone down."

If only it were the weather, she might not be so melancholy. "I have another letter for my father. I want to keep him appraised of the spring bucks."

The Marchioness lay a reassuring hand on Demeter's shoulder as she took the offered letter. "We shall send it on when these go out," she said, and added it to the pile on the table.

Then the dear woman kept right on being wonderful and kind to Demeter. "I understand you might be lonely here without purpose. Would you like to help the Dowager and I with dinner planning? We could use some assistance."

Before she knew it, she was sitting at their office table, deeply involved in sorting out who would sit near whom. They were having a dinner for everyone in the surrounding area. The reason was not exactly clear, but it didn't seem to matter. The dinner was giving them something to look forward to, and the topic of conversation would be the Prince Regent, no doubt.

The Marquess rose and kissed his wife gently on the cheek, then said something in Welsh to her belly and departed the room. Demeter mentally calculated 'right this minute' meant in around five minutes' time.

The Dowager asked, "Now, my dear, where would you like to sit?"

"Ah," uneasiness wormed into Demeter. "Why would I be sitting at the dinner table? Do I know any of the guests?"

With as little effort as she might say, "It's raining again," the Dowager said, "You're unattached you might meet a suitable gentleman and have something in common. This one is a surveyor, he is up and down the Menai researching the best place to build a bridge to Anglesey Island. He'd be an interesting one if you wanted to know about construction and the like." Then she picked up another name card and said, "This one is the overseer for a nearby estate with sheep and barley."

Reality washed over Demeter and she said, "The dinner is for introducing people ... for courtship purposes?"

The Dowager nodded. "Having purpose in one's life is deeply fulfilling. Knowing I'm helping people in their future lives does feel rather wonderful. It's high time we found you a paramour."

"But," Demeter fought the urge to flee from the room. "As you know, I am spoken for. Captain Tenby will send for me, as soon as I reply to his letters. He must have written to me, possibly to the townhouse in London - that would explain the delay!" As she said the words, she willed them to be true.

No wonder nothing had arrived for her all the way out here. He had no idea where she was, and the staff at the townhouse would be forwarding everything on to Bath, which would take several weeks most likely, and then her father would ... probably be destroying anything from Tenby.

The Marchioness gently rubbed the top of her stomach and leaned back a little. "There's no harm in coming to dinner and balancing out the men and women the table. Your father asked us to take care of you until your sisters' seasons were completed. Attending a dinner is our way of taking care of you. It is lovely having you here, by the way. It's no hardship to have one more delightful person about the house. I'm only sorry the weather hasn't been kinder to you. I'm told it is a beautiful part of the world, when the sun shines."

Demeter took a few breaths as she mentally scrambled for a reason to say no to attending the dinner.

The dowager said, "If Tenby were here, you'd both be invited. It's not as if by attending you'd be unfaithful."

Demeter *did* want to attend, if only to have something to look forward to. Attending an evening of entertainment, at her host's invitation, was unlikely to make a scandal.

"You poor love," the Dowager said, pushing back from her seat and standing up. "You need a good embrace and a willing listener. It just so happens that I can give you both."

Enveloped in the woman's warm arms, a sob burst free. "What if something's happened to him and he needs my help?"

The Dowager's embrace was a balm of kindness. "There, there, let it out."

"I miss him so much. I don't know where he is, but his situation must be dire if he hasn't sent word."

"Yes, of course," the dowager said. "Are you familiar with the writings of James Howell? 'Distance sometimes endears friendship, and absence sweetens it.' I miss my husband terribly."

Demeter leaned away in shock. "You're asking me to forget the Captain?"

The dear lady's hand shot to her sternum. "Goodness no. Just as I shall never forget my darling Gareth. Our circumstances are very different, but pining for a man who *cannot* return is not entirely dissimilar to pining for one who *will* not."

It was too much for Demeter. "You can't say Captain Tenby won't return."

The dowager shrugged and made a soft sigh. "It has been

several months. If he truly intended to marry you, he would have found a way by now."

The betrayal stung. Only moments ago, Demeter thought she had found friends who truly understood her distress.

She had to leave before she said something unforgivable. She settled on, "I need to check on the Spring doe."

CHAPTER SIX

In the stables, Demeter became more restless. The spring doe appeared to be faring well, but she still wasn't interested in drinking anything. At least in front of witnesses.

Demeter cupped her hands and filled them with water, taking them close to the doe's lips. The timid creature sniffed at her hands but was otherwise disinterested.

"You must drink," she said, "I know it's wet everywhere, but you must have water, otherwise you'll shrivel up."

A kind, familiar voice entered the barn, "She seems healthy, if a little shy."

She turned to see Mr. Alwyn at the doorway, with a thin harness in his hands.

Lightness filled her at the sight of his friendly face. "Hello, Mister Alwyn."

He raised the harness. "I made some adjustments. I thought I might take her for a walk and see if her beau is anywhere out there."

Why hadn't she thought of that? "That's a sensible idea. Would it be ... I mean, I wouldn't get in the way, but might I, ah...?"

"Would you like to join us?"

Warmth filled her. "Thank you, yes." With any luck, the rain might hold off a little. "Perhaps we should bring a second harness? We might need it if the buck returns?"

"That's sensible thinking. We are indeed fortunate to have your clear head," he said.

The compliment warmed her all the way to her toes.

A few moments later, the doe firmly harnessed, they strolled along the main road into town.

Mr. Alwyn said, "It's a shame the weather is so poorly for your visit."

"Visit?" Demeter said with no real thought. "Is that what people say I'm doing here?"

He coughed into his hand and said, "I have no right to ask, I was just assuming that's why you were here. But it is none of my business in any case."

"I should not have been so terse," Demeter said, feeling guilty at how quickly she'd rushed to speak. "The weather has made this worse than it should have been. I was sent here while my sisters attempt to find husbands. I am *persona-non-grata* and must be out of the way. I am here to learn how to think before leaping into action, as my previous actions have brought the family very low. Does that scandalize you, Mister Alwyn?"

He chuckled and his cheeks turned pink. "It does a little. My problem is I don't leap into action fast enough!"

"But you were in the army, does that not require quick thinking?"

"Well, yes, but in a different way."

On they walked, meeting people along the way who wanted to stop and chat about the unusual animal.

Mrs. Williams was most astonished and asked them, "Is this why the prince is visiting?"

Demeter blurted, "Word sure travels fast in these parts."

"It does," Mrs. Williams said. "The whole of Bangor is in a whirl to find out more. Half are saying it must be a fancy tale. But the other half says it must be real because the prince sent you a pet to look after. Now I've seen the animal for myself, I know it's real. If the animal is true, the only person who might send an animal like this out this way is probably the Prince Regent. He must be visiting us after all?"

Mister Alwyn said, "We have yet to confirm the details, but the moment we know anything, we'll let everyone else know as well."

All three nodded together. Mrs. Williams said, "I've heard there were two of them, and that the boy creature has leapt to freedom."

Mister Alwyn laughed at that. "There's no fooling you, Mrs. Williams. He has indeed. We are hoping that this doe can pick up his scent. If you hear strange noises across the fields, it could be these two calling out to each other."

Mrs. Williams wished them the best of luck in finding the buck. "Enjoy your walk now that the rain's stopped."

The rain had stopped. How unusual that Demeter hadn't noticed. Instead, she'd been so intent on walking the doe, she'd kept her focus on the animal instead of the sky. The easy conversation with Mister Alwyn had also provided a welcome distraction.

Lloyd Alwyn had heard some of the whispers about Miss Mellingham, but hadn't given them much credit. But it did seem true she'd been sent away in some kind of disgrace. Did her heart yearn for another? That could well be the case.

Be honest with yourself. You seek her company.

A familiar sense of past failure nagged at him. He'd been too slow in his younger days and missed his chance with a lady who'd captured his heart. He'd kept waiting for the right time to say something, but by the time he built up the courage, her family had posted the banns.

If they remained walking along the road, they'd be distracted by people they encountered. He'd have less chances to talk with Miss Mellingham and they'd also be far less likely to encounter the spring buck.

"Why don't we take her down toward the Menai?" He said. "The shores have plenty of bushes and outcrops where a deer might hide."

"Good idea," Demeter said, then gave a rueful smile, "And it might prevent us running in to any more Missers Williamses."

He chuckled at the sly joke. No doubt Mrs. Williams was busy telling everyone about seeing the spring doe, and the two of them.

The spring doe trotted on her spindly legs through the undergrowth, barely getting her legs wet on the long soggy grass.

His boots, on the other hand, became soaked, along with the bottom of his long pants. Demeter's dress hem was also dark from mud and dampness. At least they were only wet around their feet, which was so much better than normal.

The wind blew gently in their faces, making it easier to see what was up ahead.

The doe suddenly leapt on the spot, then let out a bizarre cry. To his surprise, Demeter kept her cool and also kept her end of the harness strings firmly in her gloved hands.

Sensible woman.

Demeter then said in a soft voice, "What is it, girl?"

The doe let out another strangled cry, sounding to Lloyd like a cross between a goat and a cat. Before he could speak his astonishment, the doe cried out again and bounced forward, taking Demeter with her.

Demeter kept pace as best she could. Lloyd chased after both of them. To her credit, she kept her grip firmly on the strings and did not let go. The doe tried to leap forward but the harness and Demeter held her firmly. After another half minute of tussle and running, the doe stopped.

Demeter, puffed and breathing heavily, turned to Lloyd and grinned.

Sparks flew in his head at such an arresting sight.

She said, "Did you see him?"

"See what?"

"The buck!"

Oh dear. He'd been too busy looking at Demeter as she kept pace with the doe. Sure enough, only a few yards ahead of them, stood the buck.

It called out to the doe in an ear-curdling reply.

Demeter laughed at their success in tracking him down.

Lloyd's knees turn to water as he realized how hopelessly he was falling for this captivating young woman.

Chapter Seven

Lloyd halted in his tracks as his eyes met the spring buck's across the grass. Earlier training took over, the training when he'd assisted with a hunt. By huge luck, they were downwind of their quarry so he hadn't sniffed their approach. However, now they could see each other, he wished mightily for some good hounds to help in the situation.

However, they were not hunting for food, and the hounds would be terribly confused at not being allowed to bring their quarry down.

Every nerve in his body urged Miss Mellingham to be quiet. To his delight and surprise, she instinctively knew to say nothing. Perhaps she'd surreptitiously joined a hunt in seasons past? No chance to ask that outright.

Instead, she lowered herself to the ground and loosened the leading strings enough to let the spring doe take a few steps forward.

He followed her lead and sat himself down into the damp grasses. He could no longer see the buck, but the doe's rear end jittered and skittered on the ground. Her tail flicked back and forth at a great rate.

Turning his head to Miss Mellingham, he noticed she eased her grip in the strings again, giving the doe a longer lead so she may get closer to the buck.

He grinned and hoped she could see how impressed he was with her. She was getting the doe closer, but still fully in control, easing the strings between her hands, always with one hand firmly holding them. The end of the strings were somewhere underneath her bottom. As long as she sat there, the doe could not go far.

It was hard to see the doe now, as the long grasses shielded most of her body.

Suddenly the buck sprang into the air in a graceful yet strange move. Its feet were tucked underneath itself as if it were … well, showing off.

Heat burned up his neck in realization. The buck most likely was showing off to the female. Any moment now Miss Mellingham would see something absolutely not fit for a lady!

If they moved from their hiding position, the buck might escape.

The creature pronged and pranced, visible high above the long grass for moments at a time before landing again.

To his surprise, the doe began walking back toward Miss Mellingham, and she in turn felt the difference in the strings' tension and began reeling her in.

She turned to Lloyd and whispered, "Let's go back."

Quietly and steadily, to not scare the doe, they rose from behind the grasses and started walking back to the stables. Every few yards, he cast a glance back to see the doe being compliant. What a clever woman Miss Mellingham was, to build such trust with the doe in such a short time frame.

She kept her voice low and asked, "Is the buck still behind?"

"It most certainly is," he confirmed.

The buck drifted farther behind at one point, but he hoped if they maintained a steady pace, the doe would lead the buck home.

Miss Mellingham said, "Mister Alwyn, if you might get to the stables first and open some of the doors for us. I can lead the doe back in and the buck might follow."

Blisteringly smart woman, he thought. "We'll then close the doors behind him."

"Precisely. I'm glad you can read my mind," she said.

Lloyd was grateful she could not read his.

It might not work, and the buck might scare off once again, but as Demeter walked the spring doe into the mostly empty barn, bar a few horses safely sheltered in their stables, she couldn't help feeling the hardest part of luring the buck home was accomplished. If he took fright and ran off, he would at least still know where the doe was, and could possibly be lured home.

"Good girl," she cooed as she took the doe back to her quarters and offered her an apple branch. Wasting no time, she tied the strings to the post and left the doe alone. The small door was open ajar, and she slipped out that way. At the last moment, she looked back to see the buck standing in the open doorway, sniffing the air, ears flicking back and forth.

Outside, Demeter found the rest of the stable hands were waiting for her - and waiting for instructions.

"You need to be incredibly quiet. Let the buck wander in and find the doe, then slowly close the doors. No sudden movements, is that clear?"

They nodded or said a low "Yes miss."

Mr. Alwyn beamed at her and said, "You're a natural leader."

It was a strange and yet welcome compliment, warming Demeter with satisfaction. "Thank you, but we're not there yet."

Every minute stretched like an hour as they held back, waiting and watching the buck as he nervously paced at the doorway, neither going in nor running away. At last he moved in a few steps. The men still held back from closing the doors. They'd listened to her instructions and were not scaring the creature away.

How refreshing to have people who listened to her!

Several tense minutes later, the buck moved directly into the barn and the men formed a line of bodies as they closed the doors and captured the buck.

Mister Alwyn held up his thin harness that was meant for the buck, should they have the opportunity. "I should give you this, you have the best chance of fitting it to him as any of us."

She nodded and took the light harness and made her way back into the barn via the small door. Mr. Alwyn followed her in and secured the door behind them.

They found the buck in close proximity to the doe. To Demeter's embarrassment and shock, the buck mounted the doe.

Mr. Alwyn said, "Oh dear."

Demeter realized it was an opportunity. "Quick, while he's distracted."

Working silently as a team, they crept up on either side of the rutting buck and slipped the harness under him. He tried to get away but Demeter held his horns sideways against her body and Mr. Alwyn made quick work of the fasteners.

Then Demeter caught sight of something she really shouldn't in the springbuck's underbelly, and felt her body aflame.

She couldn't stop staring at the protuberance.

CHAPTER EIGHT

May 25, 1816
Bangor Hall,
Dear Sir,
It is with the greatest respect that I introduce myself, Lt Colonel (ret.) Lloyd Alwyn. I have become acquainted with your daughter, Demeter, and wish to court her, with your permission.
I recommend the Marquis of Caernarfonshire as a reference, as I am in his employ.
Yours,
Alwyn.

Lloyd sealed the letter with wax and gave the footman a coin for his troubles. There was still the issue of Miss Mellingham's heart, and whether it belonged to another. If that was the case, there was no point proceeding. Surely luck would be on his side this time? Otherwise he'd look at signing up again. There was bound to be a war on somewhere…

Such a feeling of achievement flowed through Demeter, at her retrieval of the spring buck. She loved repeating the story, to anyone who would stand still for half a minute. She left out the part about the buck becoming amorous with the doe the moment they were in the stalls. That part of the story was simply too much!

The Marchioness said to her, "It is so lovely to see you smiling again, my dear. You have brought a little ray of sunshine to our gloomy part of the world."

Demeter happily spent an afternoon helping the dowager with menus and seating arrangements.

The dowager sighed as she looked at the available supplies. "We had hoped for more fruit but the best we can get is rhubarb. What goes well with rhubarb?"

"Ordinarily, apples," Demeter said, "although they are not ripe yet. Plums, perhaps? Honey? No, wait, parsnips, but baked in honey."

"- Genius!" The dowager embraced her in a firm hug. "I am ever so grateful that you are here to help my addle-pated brain!"

Demeter looked at the dowager and wondered if the woman was really as old as she was making out. She certainly looked much younger than her dear Mama. Which took her thoughts down an old path of inquiry. "Have we had any letters from my parents?"

"Nothing at all," the Dowager said, more interested in swapping name cards around on a sheet of imaginary tables. "And we've heard nothing back from court either. I am starting to wonder if you father may have misspoken?"

Possible, but then the spring buck and *doe* had arrived. Who else could they be from but the prince regent.

"Perhaps my father sent the animals here, as a way of giving me responsibility. He said I had to prove myself before he would let me return home."

They puzzled together and read her father's last letter again, trying to match what they knew for certain with what he'd written. Had they completely misread his note? The fact the animals and the price were only mentioned towards the very end had Demeter wondering if they'd read far too much into his note.

"One thing is for certain," Demeter said, "Dinner is very much going to happen and one exchanged ingredient for sweets is hardly going to save it. What else do we have?"

The Dowager sighed and said, "A lot of fish, fresh from the Menai."

They both giggled a little at the lack of variety. "What herbs do you have?"

"Plenty of those. I was thinking of making parsley and potato soup as one course, and another of fennel bulbs, quartered, cooked in milk. But we have more fish and I don't want to combine them or there will be less courses."

The planning went on four several happy hours, at which point the light from the windows grew so dim they needed candles.

When the clock struck four, the dowager turned to Demeter and said, "I must congratulate you. Three hours of dinner party planning and you haven't asked once about your absent captain."

That took her by surprise. "Goodness, really?"

"Indeed. You didn't ask about any correspondence at breakfast either. Is it possible your heart is healing from the loss?"

"Well, I mean. It's simply that, ah, I have enjoyed myself that I ..." she let the thought trail off. "Does that mean I don't love him anymore? Am I that un-constant?"

Her eyes drifted to the seating arrangements where she spotted Alwyn's name.

The Dowager's gaze followed her line of sight. "Could it be a new hero has entered the picture?"

Heat roared up Demeter's neck at the discovery.

CHAPTER NINE
JUNE 1, 1816

If anyone noticed the lack of variety in the courses at dinner, nobody mentioned it - or at least, not within Demeter's hearing.

At the head of the table, the Rosstrevors sat together, looking relaxed and happy. Everyone would have understood if Lady Amelia had not attended. She was growing scandalously large and yet remained in public. Not that Demeter had that much of a clue about such things. She remembered how large the sheep had grown at the family's summer house, and how they happily trotted around despite being wider than they were tall. Then there were the cats living in the barn, who still caught mice and rats even while their bellies scraped along the ground.

A voice behind her piped up. "Miss Mellingham?"

Oh dear, she'd missed everything the man beside her had said before those last two words. Guilt stole her breath for a moment, before she made a quick recovery. "I'm terribly sorry, I missed the question."

"No matter," the man said. He was the Baron of Abergavenny. Demeter knew who he was before they'd been formally introduced. She'd placed his name, and that of his new Duchess, in the seating positions. Recently married, he posed no danger to Demeter of forming any attachments. His wife was the Marchioness's aunt, and was here to stay for as long as required.

Abergavenny said, "Alwyn here says you charmed the wild beast into following you into the barn. Do tell!"

A welcome frisson of pride had Demeter quirking her lips. How lovely to be known as someone who could charm exotic animals, rather than the silly chit who ruined her family.

"It was a rather jolly thing," Demeter replied, enjoying the retelling to a new audience. "We were fortunate to be downwind of the spring buck, so we were much closer than anticipated by the time we locked eyes."

This was turning out to be more relaxed dinner than Demeter had anticipated. It appeared that the rules of speaking to one's left during one course, and to the right during another, no longer applied. Within moments, she was fielding friendly questions from left and right, and even diagonally. Before she knew it, Demeter had half the table's delighted attention. It felt natural to share the storytelling duties with Mr. Alwyn. After all, he was a major assistance in the animal's recovery.

Alwyn added tension to the tale. Everybody knew they'd caught the beast, but the way he relayed the events had Demeter and the rest of the table in raptures.

Alwyn said, "You should have seen Miss Mellingham, a natural Diana of the hunt. A step ahead of her quarry at all times."

The praise earned her a gentle round of applause from everyone nearby.

The Baroness of Abergavenny asked, "When might I see these marvelous creatures?"

Demeter looked up to the head of the table, and noticed their hosts had slipped away. "I'm sure the Rosstrevors won't mind if we see the animals now."

Alwyn extended the invitation to the rest of the guests, as several more wanted to see the spring bucks.

With half of the household in tow, they made mostly-dry progress to the stables. Potholes full of water were still an issue. Mr. Alwyn watched the barn door to make sure the buck didn't try another escape, while Demeter lead people over to where the buck and doe were harnessed in their shelter.

People crowded around and made soft 'ooh' and 'aww' noises, as befitting such tender beasts. As if under a spell of the creature's making, everyone remained quiet and reverential.

Whispered questions soon flowed: "What do they eat" and "can they pull a buggy"

Another favorite was "Are they cold?" which everyone agreed was probably self-evident, as they appeared to be shivering.

"Where are they from?" was soon followed by "Can you eat them?" at which point Demeter gasped and said, 'most definitely not!'

Demeter delighted in giving answers - where she could - but then became completely stumped when the baron asked, "When is the Prince Regent coming?"

Chapter Ten

June 25, 1816
Bangor Hall
North Wales

Dearest Papa,
I can hardly comprehend my change in circumstance, and so quickly.
Thanks to the arrival of the spring buck and doe from the Prince Regent,
I find myself at the center of local attention. Fear not, father, it is a glad
tiding that strangers deliver me, not condemnation for any perceived
wrongs.
This could, in fact, turn the tide of public opinion for our family. You
and Mama must come and visit - it is apparently summer now and I do
hope the sun might break through. The grass is growing but not much
else seems to want to. Certainly, anything requiring a flower to produce
has completely failed. I do miss apricots so! We are stewing parsnips
with honey and pretending they are fruit. Mixing them with rhubarb
does help, somewhat. How I do go on about crops these days! I have
become quite bucolic.
The Rosstrevors have sent correspondence to the Prince Regent to ascer-
tain when he might visit us here, to check upon his livestock. We have

heard nothing in return at this point. The animals are in robust health, although they do not seem to drink, which is truly remarkable. To make sure they do not die of thirst, I have instructed the stable hands to dip the apple branches in water before placing them in the stall. The thick, green grass is always wet, so there's no risk of them desiccating.

It reminds me of that saying, 'You can lead a horse to water, but you cannot make him drink.' Add spring bucks to that idiom as well, for they show no interest at all in their drinking trough.

How is Mama, and how do my sisters fare in their season? I pray daily there is good news, if only for Mama's nerves (and yours vicariously).

yours, Demeter

ps, if you are able to visit, would it be a hardship to bring some fruit? We cannot find any for love nor money, and I was thinking that as Bath is such a larger place, there may be some there?

Demeter buttered several slices of toast and ate them with a slosh of tea. If any correspondence had arrived for her, she had no time to ask for it, let alone read it. People were already arriving near the stables to see the strange and unusual animals.

Mister Alwyn met her by the stable doors and together they acknowledged the visitors who milled about. Mister Alwyn said, "We put up a sign at the front gate that visits don't begin until eight o'clock, but they have arrived early on their own accord."

Performing a quick count of people, Demeter reached twenty-three. They would not all fit in the stables at once. Another clutch of visitors was walking up the long drive to add to their number.

"Perhaps we should create tickets, with allotted times on them, so that the spring bucks aren't overwhelmed?"

Mister Alwyn nodded and said, "good idea," before facing the gathered visitors. "Thank you for coming. Now, these lovely creatures are shy and we don't want to scare them or harm them. Miss Mellingham will take five people at a time in to see them and -"

The gathered visitors surged to get closer to Demeter and the short door. "Be gentle!" she begged them. "There is plenty of time for all if everyone is patient."

One of the visitors said, "I've come down from Conwy." Another said, "I've been waiting for an hour!" Another grumpy man said, "I spent yesterday travelling all the way from Holyhead and was nearly caught in The Swellies coming across."

Panic made breathing difficult. The stories they told, the distances they'd come! They were understandably tired and impatient.

"Bring the animals out so we can all see them," one woman called out.

Demeter said, "We can't, they'll escape and leap the hedge."

"Leap the hedge?" The disbelieving man from Holyhead complained, "Do they have springs instead of legs or something?"

"Pretty much. That's possibly how they earned their names. Now," she added some extra oomph into her voice, "Everybody must be calm, I shall choose the five quietest people first and take them in first."

At the edge of her vision, she saw Mister Alwyn beaming with pride.

She had to admit, she was feeling pretty pleased with herself at this moment, but the sight of his approval made her heart flip.

The crowd hushed at this demand, and stopped bickering. The Holyhead man took his hat off and bowed his head reverently. Good, he could be sensible. Not that she had any clue where Holyhead was - it could be south of London for all she knew - but he seemed genuinely remorseful.

Selecting five people, including the Holyhead man, she led them into the quiet stables and firmly closed the door behind her.

Chapter Eleven

Lloyd schooled his features as he handed the servant a coin and accepted the letter. The moment he was safely unobserved, he opened the message.

> *Penrose House*
> *Bath*
> *June 10*
> *Dear Mr. Alwyn,*
> *What a novelty it is to be asked permission ahead of a disgrace, instead of forgiveness after the event. Take this as my permission to court Demeter, but her mother and I would like to attend the wedding, should a wedding eventuate.*
> *Yours,*
> *Mellingham.*

To receive a positive response - and so quickly - cleared any hurdles that lay in his path.

Now, to plan the campaign to win her heart.

For the next few days, the crowds did not abate. Working in tandem, Demeter and Mister Alwyn devised a token system - and a timing system - to make the visits run more smoothly. And safely for the animals' welfare.

Around lunch time, Demeter's stomach rumbled. Freshly-baked bread aromas greeted her as she escorted another group out of the stables.

The next clutch of visitors arrived and solved the mystery - they had a basket of pork pies. An enterprising tradesman and his wife had noted the increased traffic and was selling them from a wagon by the main road.

Tired from standing all morning, voice croaking from speaking to so many new people, Demeter asked two of the stable lads if they would assume her role so she might get some food herself.

One of the lads smiled broadly upon accepting his new position. "If you're hungry, Miss, there are Pork Pies by the main gate, and mussels down at the jetty."

Her mouth watered at the thought. She turned to Mister Alwyn and said, "You deserve some food and rest."

"Mussels do sound like a grand idea, give me a minute." He then availed himself of some more stable hands to take on his role of keeping the visitors in order.

* * *

• • •

Sunshine filled Lloyd Alwyn's spirits, even though the drizzle kept on swirling. The concept of food wagons filled his head with possibilities. Would he be able to track down the mess cook and entice him to create and sell food? Tricky proposition, though. It had to be something people could eat with their hands. He did begin to wonder how people were to eat mussels and not make a mess of their clothes. As he turned his collar up against the wet, he began to wonder if they should sell umbrellas as well?

The mussel stall at the jetty had solved the tableware issue - they were using small metal bowls, which reminded him of army mess halls. The aromas greeted them long before they joined the already established queue of hungry people. He made a mental note that the Rosstrevors might allow the household kitchen staff to sell crempogs too. They always went down so well, and ... oh, but jam was in short supply, so they'd have to be plain. He quite forgot himself and realized the Rosstrevors should probably avoid anything to do with trade. That didn't mean the staff couldn't make a little extra on the side.

The queue moved on and at last he and Demeter paid for and received their bowl of mussels. The drizzle didn't matter so much, as they stood under an oak tree that offered a little respite.

Shellfish could be tricky to the uninitiated, but the way Demeter delicately cracked the top shell away and ate the mussel with a delicate slurp did strange things to him.

Best concentrate on his own food, as his stomach rumbled in anticipation.

Munching companionably together, they soon finished their meal and drank the remaining broth, rich with leeks and herbs.

"My goodness, I could eat another bowl immediately," Demeter said.

"You'd fit right in in the army," Lloyd said. Quite why he'd said that flummoxed him.

Demeter smiled broadly, a tiny green spot of herb stuck between her teeth. "I hope that was a compliment!"

He nearly tripped over his tongue in haste. "Yes, of course," he said. "Ah, and there's also a little, ah, green..."

A wafted finger at his own teeth should help her find it.

She found it. "How vexing. Ruined the perfect moment," she said, as she turned away and removed it.

Desperately not wanting to look and make the moment any more awkward than it need be, Lloyd turned his own bowl over to see if there were any makers markings on the bottom.

"Well I'll be!" He exclaimed. "These *are* ex-army stock! I thought my mind was playing tricks on me."

In which case, he really should get ahold of the old army cook, because someone was already muscle-ing in to a lucrative little market. He smiled at his own amusement.

When Demeter turned back, he held his hand out for her bowl and shells to return them to the seller.

The queue was longer than before, as people walked down from the stables, and more visitors arrived at the jetty from across the strait. It could be a boon for all concerned to cater for so many customers.

He handed the bowls to a woman stirring a large pot and she nodded her thanks at their return. Lloyd said, "they were delicious, thank you for a most excellent repast!"

The woman colored a little and said, "I'm only stirring the pot, the one you want to thank is heading here just now with more mussels."

Indeed, a man only a year or so younger than he was walking up from the jetty with a crate of mussels, so fresh the seawater was still dripping off them.

"As I live and breathe," Lloyd said upon seeing his face.

The man put down his crate and stood tall, saluting Lloyd. "Corporal Alwyn, Sir!"

"What an incredible stroke of luck. I was just thinking this endeavor would be perfect for you. Sure as eggs, here you are."

Demeter reached his side at that point. She turned to the man with the mussels, but instead of appearing pleased with her deli-cious vittles, she had turned white as stone.

One hand pressed against her sternum as she gasped. "Captain Tenby? What are you doing here?"

To Lloyd's bewilderment, the cook abandoned the crate of mussels, ran straight back to the jetty and then leapt into a coracle.

He paddled urgently into the waters, but the rounded, one-man boat refused to be rushed.

Whatever was the matter with the man? Everyone knew cora-cles needed a gentle hand on the oar, not brute strength! Had the man learned nothing of Alwyn's lessons in Welsh living?

Chapter Twelve

Demeter could not think.

Far too many confusing happened far too quickly.

It was Tenby. Of that she was sure. Tenby; alive and well and deeply involved in the food trade. Tenby; had recognized her and panicked.

But why? Should the man not be glad to see her, after all this searching?

Tenby had only moments earlier saluted Mister Alwyn, so they must have known each other from their army days. Unless her Captain Tenby had a twin who was also in the services?

That made the least sense of all.

Just as the eager visitors to the springbucks had tested her patience these past few days, this latest event sorely tried Demeter's temperament.

Perhaps her captain was embarrassed - and he should be at this moment, with such poor rowing prowess on display. Out in the waters of the Menai Strait, Captain Tenby, decorated war hero, thrashed about and sent himself in spirals.

He'd been a decorated war hero, yet now he was serving food by the river? Such a come-down from his previous status. Is that why he was so embarrassed? Had word reached the wider community of their failure to marry?

Until now, Demeter had thought society only punished women, but perhaps Tenby was living with the wrath of society's disapproval?

As she and Mr. Alwyn walked closer to the jetty, her former paramour sent himself in what must be nauseatingly tight circles.

Mister Alwyn asked her, "Why did you call him Tenby?"

There was so little room for more confusion in Demeter's mind, yet Mr. Alwyn had managed to add a little more. Indignant heat rose up her neck and she said, "I called him Tenby, because that is his name."

The confused expression on Mr. Alwyn's face sent coldness plummeting through Demeter's belly. It added to her entire discombobulation to be hot and cold at the same time.

Mister Alwyn shook his head and said, "He is the cook from the army days. As numbers dwindled in his regiment, we co-opted him into ours. Everyone knew him as Smith. Is Tenby his Christian name?"

Should Demeter faint or cast up her accounts? The strength in her knees turned soft and she had to lean on a post beside the jetty to hold herself upright. "I know him as Captain Tenby, but I am starting to think that might be a lie."

If his name was a lie, what else had been a lie? That he loved her? That they were destined to marry?

Meanwhile, the man who had spirited her toward Gretna Green in such haste was at this moment spinning out of control as the tides dragged his little boat southwards.

"There was a Tenby," Mr. Alwyn said, "Now that I think about it. He died in battle." His voice dropped to just below a whisper. "There were a lot of letters to write that day to soldiers' families."

Movement caught the corner of her eye as the woman stirring the vat of mussels picked up Tenby's abandoned crate of shellfish.

The people surrounding the jetty began shouting out to the

man on the boat, trying to give him instructions to steer better. Another threw a rope out to him, but it was wildly short of its mark.

Through the hubbub, Mr. Alwyn said, "He's passed out."

"He's what?"

Mr. Alwyn sprang into action. In a flash he dropped his hat and coat, then charged down the jetty shouting, "Clear the way!" At speed, he reached the end of the timbers and dove off the end into the swirling waters.

With bold strokes, he swam with the current towards the incapacitated Tenby.

Demeter grabbed his hat and coat off the wet grass, carrying them as she jogged along the shores of the strait, keeping an eye on them while also watching out for tripping hazards.

Heart beating hard, she prayed for Mr. Alwyn's strength and vigor as he slowly closed the distance to Tenby's little round boat.

More people began jogging alongside the river, shouting out encouragement to Mr. Alwyn.

Nearly, nearly!

Alwyn reached for the lip of the boat but his arm wasn't long enough. A few more strokes and he was nearly there. Meanwhile Tenby remained oblivious to the chaos around him.

A runner near Demeter said something about stopping them before they reached The Swellies, or they'd both be done for.

Puffed and barely keeping up, Demeter couldn't ask what any of that meant.

Mr. Alwyn reached the boat and had his hand on the lip of it. Thank heavens he no longer had to swim!

He splashed water over Tenby's face to rouse him. People running along the riverside cheered and called out.

The man who'd mentioned The Swellies had a coil of rope in his hand. He ran ahead much farther, getting ahead of the current.

Meanwhile, Mr. Alwyn clung to the side of the boat, using his long body as a trailing anchor to help guide the coracle closer to the riverbank. Her esteem for the man rose so high, Demeter thought she might swoon.

This was the behavior of a hero.

As long as he lived, of course. There were already enough dead heroes on the battlefield, including whoever the real Tenby was.

Of course, it started raining again.

She could endure a little wet, considering what Mr. Alwyn was going through.

Up ahead, the man who'd had the rope positioned himself on an outcrop a little further downriver. He called out to Mr. Alwyn to get his attention. Heart in her mouth she watched the man throw the rope to Mr. Alwyn's free hand.

It missed.

Damn!

Lightning fast, the man pulled the wet rope back and tried again. This time it landed true and Mr. Alwyn grabbed it tightly.

Demeter's legs gave out and exhaustion took her down.

Lloyd was a fool. He'd missed his chance - just as he had all those years ago. Not only that, he'd gone and rescued the very man who threatened his future happiness with Demeter!

He should have left Smith to his folly, but something about the hapless situation had him leaping into the water.

What blastedly awful timing!

Dragging the lifeless Smith to the banks, several people stepped in to assist and help them both to their feet. It was a messy journey back to the big kitchens of the big house, as he squelched and slopped his way there.

Smith came 'round part of the way back. He spluttered something about being alive and being so grateful. But Lloyd didn't care for gratitude when it meant he'd lost his chance with Demeter.

Despite this, he couldn't bring himself to be angry at either of them. He'd never exactly discovered whether Demeter still yearned for this charlatan.

His only hope lay in Demeter coming to her senses, but she was being assisted back to the big house as well. He held onto hope that she might have fainted at his bravery, but it was far more likely that she'd been overcome at seeing her love again after all this time.

Once again, he'd waited too long and lost.

Long after the excitement settled after such a commotion, Demeter sat in the kitchen, drinking sweet tea by the fire.

The hat and coat Demeter had carried for Mr. Alwyn were hanging near the fire to dry. His boots too were peeled open and upturned on the hearth. Judging by the puddles on the stones, they would take a while to be ready to wear again.

Her emotions roiled as she took in the faces of those around her.

The expression on Mr. Alwyn's face was full of gentle concern when he looked her way, and righteous fury when he turned to Tenby. Steam rose from his drying clothes as he shifted a blanket about himself.

Captain Tenby had the decency to appear ashamed, but he possibly had a fair amount of nausea to recover from as well, what with all the spinning.

Sipping tea at the same table was the Dowager Marchioness. This surprised Demeter as she thought the lady would have far more pressing concerns, such as the next dinner and the health of her daughter-in-law.

The dowager placed her cup into the saucer with a firm clunk and asserted herself. "Let's get down to business, who are you really?" She asked the man who couldn't bring himself to look Demeter's way.

"My real name is Smith, and I was a cook for the regiments."

Smith sighed but still did not look to Demeter. "When the war was over, I had but a life of drudgery to return to, so I took Tenby's name instead. Wasn't like he needed it anymore."

The callous use of a dead man's reputation burned acid in Demeter's throat. She'd been such a poor judge of true character. Worse than that, her father had been right! Tenby *was* so unsuitable!

The Dowager spoke again. "I see no respectable way out of this but that you should marry Miss Mellingham. However, if you go back to Smith, you will be denying her any place in society. It's not right that she be punished for your deception."

Still he did not look at Demeter.

This was too much for her, and she clenched her fists. "Do I get a say in the matter?" She asked the room.

Mr. Alwyn and the lady turned to her. The dowager said, "By all means."

"Good," Demeter hoped her twisting stomach would not interrupt proceedings. This was no rush to judgement on her part, rather, the hideous realization of wasting months of emotions on a man who did not deserve it. "I do not wish to marry that man, whether he goes by Tenby or Smith. If that means I remain a spinster the rest of my years, so be it. I foolishly believed the lies he told me, at the time, including that he would support and love me. But his actions today in abandoning his duties at the first sign of difficulty show how utterly unsuitable he was and would be. Who's to say he won't drop me like a crate of wet mussels at the next sign of troubles?"

Saying the words reinforced Demeter's resolution that she would rather die an old maid than be shackled to a man with no backbone.

Smith spoke up, and this time he *almost* looked at Demeter. "I was in shock, that is all."

Mr. Alwyn scoffed and said, "You weren't so shocked to see me. It was only when Miss Mellingham appeared that you turned and ran. I'll take her word over yours any day."

Something warm unfurled in Demeter at Mr. Alwyn's declaration.

"Now, now," the dowager said, as a smile crept into her cheeks. "No name calling required. Smith, how lucrative is the mussel trade that you are now engaged in?"

He shrugged and said, "It might go very well, provided people keep coming to visit those bouncing deers in the stables."

Was that a twinkle in the dowager's eyes? The woman certainly appeared pleased with herself. "Good," she said. "The springbucks will be here for the foreseeable future. I am developing an enterprise, it involves dinner parties and will also include a visit to the springbucks for all guests. I want mussels on the menu, and from what I heard, yours were delicious. This could be your path to redemption and an honest living. Are you interested?"

Demeter butted in, "Am I not responsible for the spring bucks? And now I must maintain the animals in order to continue a business endeavor between the two of you?"

The dowager's soft smile eased her worries as she said, "The spring bucks are central to this, but there's no need for the two of you to cross paths at all. However, I will require a reliable supply of food if these dinners are to be a success." She turned her attentions to Smith and demanded, "Are you able to obtain good quantities in an honest manner?"

Smith nodded slowly at first, then more rapidly as his mind seemed to catch up with the rest of the discussion and how lightly he was escaping their wrath.

"Good," the dowager said. "Then, let's talk terms."

For the next little while, Demeter felt nothing but confusion as the Dowager ignored Mr. Alwyn and herself and talked of business with Mr. Smith.

July 6, 1816

Dearest Father,

you were correct.

There, I have committed those words to paper. 'You were correct.'

Captain Tenby was utterly unsuitable for me. He has finally arrived, and I have seen his true nature.

For the rest of my days you may say, 'I told you so,' and I shall agree that you did tell me so, and that I did not listen.

In retrospect, I am glad the axel broke and we did not wed. I know that not marrying is a worse scandal than marrying an unsuitable man, but when I have enough paper and time, I will explain everything to you and Mama.

Meanwhile, the springbucks are drawing people from near and far, keen to see these majestic creatures for themselves. A local artist has drawn their likeness, which I enclose. He has not quite captured how thin their legs are. I believe he is more used to drawing horses. He is now living in the stables so that he can capture their true forms at a moment's notice.

I do have an earnest request. I should like to remain in Bangor.

There is another shock for you. I am not asking this to be contrarian, I truly have grown to admire the place and the people. Even the rain! Can you credit it? My earlier correspondence was full of pleas to bring me home, but I have since discovered this area suits me to a nicety. Spinsterhood also suits me and I shall be happy to live out my years in that state.

The Dowager Marchioness and I are busy preparing for the Prince Regent's eventual visit, although we have no confirmation of his arrival date, or of his arrival at all. No correspondence has arrived on that point.

Do you have news of this? It would greatly assist the planning of events in this part of Wales if we knew when to expect his majesty.

Your daughter,

Demeter

ps, please extend my best wishes to mother and my sisters. I hope they have fully recovered from the shame I have brought to the family. Who knew six months of rain and a pair of springbucks would bring me to my senses?

Chapter Thirteen
July 10, 1816

The rain was in full flow again, paying absolutely no heed to the calendar. Demeter pulled her cloak over her head as she walked to the stables. So many people arrived every day, wanting to meet the animals. When it drizzled, they stood out in the open. Heavy rain had them huddling under umbrellas or standing under the eaves of the big house.

The stable hands had adapted to their new responsibilities of keeping people in line. Young Roberts was especially keen. Thank goodness for reliable people. Perhaps, with a little more training, they could take over the running of the visitors? Then Demeter could better spend her time doing … hmmm, doing what exactly? If she was not tending the springbucks, what role did she have with the Rosstrevors? Arranging dinners with the dowager had lost its appeal now that they would be dealing with Smith to supply ingredients. The thought of having to see him, even if briefly, held no appeal at all.

"I am a spinster now," she told herself, "So I may as well act like one."

When she entered the stables, she found the springbucks

safely in their shelter. They had obviously been steadily eating, judging by the number of droppings in the straw by their feet. At some point they'd need to move the springbucks to another stall so the stable boys could get in there and muck it out.

This would be a special treat for the visitors, to help move the animals to another stall. Demeter asked the crowd, "As you're all so quiet and respectful, I wonder if any of you could help move the springbucks to another stall?"

Everyone's hands rose, and she felt a warm glow.

Roberts spoke up. "I'll do it, miss!"

The guests softly groaned at missing out. One reached into his pocket and brought out a coin. Oh goodness, they were willing to pay to perform an action that was normally left to the staff.

Extraordinary!

The sand in the egg-timer emptied, so she asked the group to move on so that more visitors could have their turn.

The man who'd held up a coin then asked, "Is their manure for sale? I'd wager it's a tonic for the kitchen garden."

Goodness, this felt scandalously close to being in trade, but it was an opportunity too good to pass up. "I can sell you a sack and one of the boys will fill it for you."

Mr. Alwyn made his way into the stables.

Heat rose up her cheeks as if she were sitting by the fire in the kitchen.

He walked over to her and said, "Miss Mellingham, I hoped you would be here."

Nerves assailed her, and she had to think of something to say. "They need names," she said, pointing to the animals. "Chaos and Mayhem might suit."

Mr. Alwyn grinned and added, "What about Panda and Monium?"

This gave Demeter a giggle. "Topsy and Turvey?" She suggested.

"Oh yes, that's hit the target," he said.

A messy silence descended, making things feel so much more complicated than they needed to.

"It has been remiss of me," she said, "I must thank you for your heroics in the river. I owe you a great deal of thanks."

The current group of visitors exited the stables and a fresh group entered.

He cleared his throat and said, "Why don't we take a walk to the front gate and put up the closed sign? We can give Topsy and Turvey the rest of the day off?"

Lucky animals to have time to themselves.

"I would be grateful for the walk, thank you," she managed.

Their steps synchronized as they walked to the gate.

A Rosstrevor footman trotted past them on a horse, as he carried the family's mail for the day.

The letter she's written to her father would be amongst it. Should she take it back? She'd never hear the end of his gloating. With a wince, she let the footman pass them and turn towards town, where he spurred the horse into a canter.

Too late to call it back now.

"You seem upset?" Mr. Alwyn said.

She sighed heavily and had to admit she was. "I wrote a hasty letter to father and admitted, in writing, that he was correct about Tenby. He will never let me live it down, of course."

Mr. Alwyn's face fell and she rushed to reassure him. "I'm sure he wants what's best for me, but I am now beginning to understand the enormous strain I have placed on the family. Which means if he wishes to remind me of my misdeeds, he is quite at liberty. I did do a dreadful thing. Goodness, this might have been easier if he'd vanished in the river. Not that I'd ever wish that on anyone."

Mr. Alwyn's voice cracked a little as he spoke. "Miss Mellingham, I would never hold that against you. I take it you are not keen to pursue anything with him?"

She blurted, "Very much not keen at all. Although you were incredibly brave to rescue him. You have my thanks for that, and everyone's."

He stopped walking and turned to her. "I'm only sorry you have to endure his presence for however long we have visitors for the springbucks."

"I'm sure I shall manage. A few bruises to my soul will heal in time."

Ringing noises filled Lloyd's ears. His timing was either perfect or too late once again. He had to press on, or he'd die wondering. "I should tell you," he said, his voice breaking a little, "I received a letter from your father recently. I was going to talk with you but … well, we've had other adventures that have kept us busy."

"You've received a letter, but I have not? How very typical of Papa. Did he confirm when the Prince Regent will be coming?"

His heart beat faster as he looked upon her face. "He singularly did not impart that pertinent fact. Possibly because I failed to ask him."

This brought Demeter up short. "So why were you writing to him at all if not to ask that?"

He took her hands in his. Flurries of confusion and anticipation spread through him. "Because, I was asking about a completely different matter. I was asking … permission to court you."

"Oh!" Demeter said.

"Oh?" He replied.

He'd rather hoped she might swoon or smile, but she appeared confused. Had he given her no indication of his affections? He thought his praise at the recent dinner had been so exuberant he would set tongues wagging.

Demeter shook her head. "Yes, 'Oh'. Because, in the letter to my father the footman is just now riding off to town with, I said I shall see out my days as a confirmed spinster."

Cold water poured down his spine. "Why would you say such a thing?"

"Well," she chewed her bottom lip. "I thought it was true. Why did you not say anything to me of your feelings?"

The rain fell harder. They sought the shelter of the oak tree where things were somewhat less damp under its broad leaves.

Lloyd said, "I wanted to tell you, but we had so many visitors. And you were terribly busy with the springbucks. Then that blackguard Smith-Tenby arrived. For a while there I wasn't sure if you still held affection for him, and if that was the case, well, I … felt I should withdraw my pursuit."

Demeter chuckled and said, "We have both let our imaginations run against us. It's true, I was surprised to see Tenby after all this time, but instead of feeling elated, I … came to my senses rather abruptly. I then doubted my ability to judge a person's character, after being so wrong about him. I truly was prepared to be a spinster, believe me, I wasn't merely saying it to rush a declaration on your part."

Their clasped hands pressed tightly together.

Hope chased away his fears. "I truly hope you do not want to be a spinster. Or at least, not for much longer?"

She blushed.

He had to take his chance. "I'd be delighted to ask you to marry me right here and now, but I don't want to rush you."

The pink on her cheeks extended to her delicate ears. "Well, if you want to ask me, you may as well go ahead, although -"

"- Miss Mellingham, will you marry me?"

A smile of something wonderful filled her face, and Lloyd could have died and gone to heaven. Gradually, her winning smile developed into something *almost* scheming.

Demeter said, "I'd be delighted to answer you, right here and now … but … I have decided *not* to rush things."

He couldn't believe she'd echoed his sentiments back to him. This was going to be a wonderful wooing. "Would asking for a kiss be rushing things?"

"Not at all," she said, and pressed her lips to his.

Her lips were soft and prefect against his. His heart crashed against his ribs with joy.

EPILOGUE
AUGUST, 1816

Mary Rosstrevor, Dowager Marchioness of Caernarfonshire, enjoyed her afternoon stroll along the banks of the Menai. She read another angry letter from Demeter's father and gave a naughty chuckle. Not that she'd withheld all the correspondence that had come from Mister Mellingham; just the more recent, terse, epistles demanding Demeter depart for Bath.

> *July 20, 1816*
>
> *Demeter,*
>
> *I cannot believe you to still be in North Wales when you should be here in Bath. Did you not receive my letters advising that you and the springbucks needed to be here by the 15th of this month for the Prince Regent's visit?*

And on it went. The letter had arrived far too late to be of any use. Even if it had been delivered with enough time, Mary would not have handed it on. Or the earlier one. The animals, Demeter and Mr Alwyn belonged here, at Bangor Hall. Her future dinner party and matchmaking plans depended upon them remaining so.

In a few deft rips, she's reduced the letter to tiny pieces. She fed them to the swirling waters and waved them farewell.

In the middle of a stable, the object of Lloyd's affection looked the very picture of satisfaction.

He couldn't help grinning at how blessed he was to be courting her. Demeter was a natural leader, the way she greeted and thanked people, never needed to raise her voice and kept things running smoothly.

The baron of Abergavenny and his baroness were visiting the springbucks today and had secured a private audience with them. The baroness noted, "The doe looks much improved. She must be enjoying the food as her belly is so lovely and round now."

As they looked to the doe, Lloyd caught a flicker of muscle across the doe's flanks. The buck became agitated, flaring his nostrils and flicking his ears.

The doe then stomped her feet and moved away from the buck, pushing herself into the corner.

Suddenly, Lloyd realized what must be going on. He reached for the buck's harness and said, "Might just take him to the other stall for safekeeping."

Walking away with the buck, he heard Demeter gasp in shock. No time to look her way, he needed to ensure the buck could not cause problems, if his suspicions about what might be happening were correct.

The baroness also drew breath and said, "I believe she might be having a … calf? Or a foal or a … what *are* their babies called?"

Demeter voice was full of wonder, "I'm not sure. I have found no books on springbuck husbandry in any libraries in these parts."

The baron said, "Perhaps that was why the prince got rid of them, because they breed quickly? I wonder how many she'll have?"

The doe's ears flicked back and forth and she appeared distressed. Clearly, she wanted freedom from her harness, but they dared not let her out because she could injure herself and the babe if she started leaping about.

The baron placed a gentle arm around his baroness and said, "I told you we'd see the sights, but I didn't realize how soon the sights would come to us!"

They both chuckled at this, looking incredibly happy. Good for them, he thought, wanting to place his arm around Demeter in the same way. Perhaps he should. They were officially courting now.

The small stable door burst open, frightening everyone. A flustered maid appeared and said to the baroness, "There you are, the lady is asking for you."

The lady righted herself and a serious expression took hold. "She hasn't started already, has she?"

The maid lowered her voice and said, "No, but, begging your pardon, she's uncomfortable and is asking for you."

The baroness gave her husband a departing kiss and said, "Poor lass, still has a month to go and is already the size of a barn."

The baroness followed the maid out to the big house, and then it was just the three of them. Lloyd racked his brains for a reason to be rid of the baron, so that he and Demeter could have some time together.

"More straw," Demeter said to nobody in particular.

Lloyd gathered extra straw and placed it into the doe's stall. In silent wonder, the three of them watched as the doe brought a little life into the world.

Eventually the little brown babe staggered onto long limbs and stood upright, it's wet brown fur a stark contrast to the mother's white belly.

The baron chuckled and said, "Let's hope he grows into those ears, otherwise he might sail away on a stiff breeze."

The ears did look comically large, but that only made the babe more endearing.

Lloyd said, "Please inform his lordship that we now have three spring bucks on the property."

The baron nodded and set off back to the house. The moment they were lone, he reached for Demeter's hand and drew her to him. She smiled and leaned in to his embrace.

Could there be a more perfect moment?

"Thank you for not rushing me, my love," Demeter said.

Warmth spread through him. He repeated her words back to her with a chuckle. "'My love', I rather enjoy the sound of that. I might start saying it back to you, from time to time."

Demeter snuggled in as she said, "I do rather enjoy this non-rushed courtship. It feels like the right time to tell you, Lloyd, I am in love with you. Not madly, of course, as that suggests a loss of common sense. I am very sensibly in love with you, in a measured, reasonable meaning of the w -"

Lloyd kissed the rest of her sentence away. For the first time in his life, his timing was perfect.

August 12, 1816

Bangor Hall

Dearest Mama and Papa

When you have stopped laughing at my expense after my previous letter, which I pray never arrived and is lost to the world, you may have further cause for mirth in my situation.

Mister Lloyd Alwyn has asked me to marry him, and I have accepted. You see, I have matured a great deal and I'm doing things in the right order these days - we shall not cause any scandal whatsoever and are happy to come to Bath for the ceremony or wait until you can journey to Bangor Hall. I hope the weather improves so that this letter, and your response to it, don't take quite so long to arrive.

Your daughter,

Demeter

I hope you had a wonderful time in North Wales with Demeter and Lloyd.

Turn the page for the first chapter of another sweet romance that follows on from this one, *All Roads Lead To Earls*.

All Roads Lead to Earls
Chapter 1

Bangor, North Wales

September, 1817

YOUR Committee have confined their inquiry to the state of the Road from London to Holyhead, and make it the subject of a separate Report, in consequence of the late period of the Session; and of the urgent necessity of some immediate effort to repair and improve that part of it which runs through North Wales.

The whole of this part of the Road is in the worst possible condition; it is exceedingly narrow (in some places but scarcely wide enough to admit two carriages to pass); and "it is carried unnecessarily over many hills, the ascents and descents of which are often one foot in height to fourteen in length, one in ten, one in eight, and even one in seven."

Besides, many parts of it are very dangerous to travellers; for where it is the most narrow and most steep, and the most interrupted by sharp turns, it passes along the side of precipices many hundred feet high, and without any other protection to carriages than small walls built of loose stones, or very low and narrow banks of earth.

According to the Estimate of Mr. Fulton, who was recently employed by the Lords Commissioners of His Majesty's Treasury to survey this Road, it appears that the sum necessary to put it into repair (without making any improvement by deviations from the present line, or lowering any of the hills) is £ 46,540. 18s. 7d. ; a circumstance which most forcibly explains how excessively bad the present condition of this Road must be.

Hannah Jones, lady's companion to the Marchioness of Caernarfonshire, thought she might pass out as she tried to envision the enormous sum her employer had just read aloud to the family gathered in the breakfast room at Rosstrevor House.

The forty-six thousand part had barely entered her brain when her head turned fuzzy with the rest of it. She reached for her tea and sipped, hoping it might help things make sense.

Sitting at the table, Amelia Rosstrevor, Marchioness of Caernarfonshire (and Hanna's esteemed employer), put the report she'd just read down on the table. Then she too reached for a cup of tea.

There were a great many people who had come to grief along that awful road. It was in a shocking state, and it did need repair. But the price? It could bankrupt the government!

The marchioness turned to her husband, sitting opposite at the table and repeated the details: "Forty-six thousand, five hundred and forty pounds, eighteen shillings and seven pence."

The Marquess of Caernarfonshire let out a low whistle at the amount. His mouth then canted with mischief. "Wherever will they get the eighteen shillings and seven pence?"

Amelia shook her head with mirth, then reached for some toast.

Hannah adored her employer and her husband, who were loving toward each other and caring toward their staff. Considering her low situation in life, Hannah had done exceptionally well for herself to become a lady's companion. She spent her time making amiable conversation and sewing, when her ladyship required her company. When not required (her ladyship was still greatly enamored of her husband, she really wasn't required for that much company) Hannah was at liberty to visit with the Alwyns and their spring bucks, who lived on the estate. The Alwyns' rare animals and their four-legged babies drew a steady stream of visitors from far and wide.

It was an idyllic life, all things considered, but Hannah was surrounded by people deeply in love with each other - even the animals had birthed another calf, or foal, or whatever they were called. Hannah couldn't help feeling, at the age of four and twenty, a little pang of jealousy that she might have missed her chance at something similar.

The Marchioness declared, "When the road is in better condition, I daresay we'll have even more visitors." She turned to her mother-in-law, also sitting at the breakfast table, playing with heir to the marquisate, Rhodri. "Lady Mary, I imagine that news excites you?"

Lady Mary, the dowager marchioness was too busy babbling to her grandson to pay them any attention.

Another pang gripped Hannah. She sternly reminded herself she could have done so much worse in life, and she should not take her current situation for granted.

Yet still, the yearning persisted. Especially when she was in the same room as young Rhodri.

The Dowager then dipped a thin slice of toast into her runny boiled egg and held it up to the pudgy babe for a taste. His eyes grew round as his tongue dabbed against the bright yellow yolk. Most of it ended up on Rhodri's chin, but some went down the right way.

Lady Rosstrevor asked her husband, "Do you think they'll begin work on the road soon?"

"They'll have to," he replied, "How else is everyone supposed to get from Dublin to London?"

Lady Mary kept up her baby-talk and helped the young heir join in the conversation. "They're also going to build a big bridge all the way over the Menai Strait! We'll be able to see it from the garden!"

The Marquess chuckled, "I don't think it will be quite that big, mother. Though I am intrigued to see what Telford comes up with."

"It will no doubt be grand if it costs forty-six thousand pounds," she replied. Then her voice rose an octave and said repeated the amount to young Rhodri. "Did you know numbers went up that high? Of course you did, you're so clever! More egg?"

One of the footmen came in with a tray of letters on a salver. He placed the tray beside the master of the house on the table.

Once the servant was out of the room, David slid the letters to Amelia and she sorted through them. She soon had two letters for herself and her husband, and six for the dowager.

"Your enterprise is coming along rather well, Lady Mary," Amelia noted.

Hannah heartily approved of the enterprise, as they called it. From time to time, the men far outnumbered the women, and she and some of the staff were able to join in, to 'balance the table'.

"It was your idea," Lady Mary said. "I'd be more than happy with your assistance any time you feel like stepping back in," she said with a pointed look.

"I'm rather enjoying my leisure," Amelia confessed.

"As you should," Mary said, standing up with young Rhodri and delivering the babe into his father's arms. "If this is how busy I am now," she said, taking up her pile of correspondence, "Imagine what life will be like once the road works really begin!"

She wasn't complaining at all. Hannah could tell by the smile in her face and the twinkle in her eyes, that she was already plotting the most wonderful match-making adventures to ever take place in this quiet little part of north Wales.

Who knew, perhaps Hannah might one day find herself matched with a caring tradesman, or even an engineer!

A woman could still dream.

November, 1817

Homesickness sapped the strength of Patrick Belconnen, the Earl of Tullamore, as his driver navigated the shockingly bad roads through the north of Wales.

Each bruising bump grew bigger with every worsening mile. The countryside itself was beautiful, in direct contrast to the quality of the roads. The land fell away precipitously at one point, and he pulled the curtains shut and leaned hard the other way, praying a little more that they'd make it around the bend alive.

Every pothole on one side of the carriage matched with a bump on the other. Just as things developed a rhythm, they would break with a series of ruts and shudders. It would be a wonder if he wasn't twisted like wet, knotty string by the time they reached Bangor.

Bangor was his next destination, but after that, he and the driver had a perilous boat journey across the Menai Strait and a day's travel before he reached Holyhead on the other side of the island of Angelsey. There, they'd take a steam packet from Holyhead to Dublin. He'd send on a letter to his family - the carriage shuddered as the left wheel dropped into rut - from Dublin and, if fortune smiled upon him, he'd be home the day after.

Crack.

That did not sound safe.

John Coachman slowed the horses down. They'd be lucky to

make Bangor at all at this rate. The days were so short and the sun had sunk low already. It must be almost four in the afternoon.

The carriage stopped, then the timbers creaked ominously as the driver stepped down. It groaned some more and he could have sworn the coachman was unhitching the horses. A knock at the door quickly followed, so he opened it.

The driver stood there with his hand stretched out to him, face pale as milk. "Take my hand immediately sir, the carriage is about to collapse."

Taking him at his word, Patrick grabbed his hand as a whooshing sound filled his ears.

The carriage tipped and swayed backwards just as he stepped out. Suddenly there wasn't a step any more, as the driver grabbed him and held him steady.

Patrick turned in time to see the carriage tumble sideways as the axel broke and a wheel shattered.

The shock quite drew his breath away, and nearly loosened his bowels at the same time.

"I'm in your debt, good man," Patrick eventually said when his senses returned from the fright.

The horses, as he'd guessed, were not attached to the carriage, so they were unharmed. Again, thanks to his coachman's quick thinking.

"There's an Inn up ahead, I hope that means we've reached Bangor," Patrick said.

With no option but to leave the carriage where it fell, they each took hold of a horse and walked into the small town. They found an inn and handed over the horses to a stable hand. The sign above the door said, "Llandygai," but was it the name of the town or the establishment itself?

Finding the innkeeper, and exchanging details of their ordeal, they learned Bangor was only another two miles down the road.

The innkeeper was devastated that he had no private rooms, "for a man of such quality," but then quickly added, "The

Rosstrevors are at the Big House in Bangor, they'd be delighted to offer you assistance. I'll get you a fresh horse."

Exhausted but relieved, Patrick arrived at a grand country seat, well-lit with torchlights to guide him to the main door. The Marquess quickly understood his predicament and set his staff to securing him a room and filling a bath.

"Was just reading about the how bad the road is the other day," the Marquess said as he guided him to a retiring room with a roaring fire and comfortable chairs.

How utterly heavenly! Then a footman arrived with an offer of whisky and he gladly accepted. "I can tell you from first-hand experience, that road is in shocking condition. If not for the quick actions of my coachman, I'd have lost my life this very day," Patrick said, his aching bones virtually melting into the comfortable furniture.

If he wasn't careful, he'd fall asleep in this very spot.

"Agreed," his host said, "Work will start soon, of that I've no doubt."

The Dowager Marchioness came in to, "inform his lordship that his bath is ready."

That was fast, Patrick thought, quickly followed by another thought; why wasn't a footman telling him this? The answer to that became readily apparent as the dowager asked him a terribly impertinent question, disguised as politeness. "Will the Countess Tullamore be joining us soon? I shall prepare rooms for her."

He nodded at hearing the question, then tilted his head in a little suspicion. "I am a bachelor, my good lady. No countess as yet, though it pains my mother so."

"In that case, you must join us for a dinner party this evening."

"You do not need to entertain on my account," he said. A hot bath awaited him, and he was looking forward to a long soak, followed by a good night's rest.

They reached the base of the stairs. The dowager was intent on leading him to his rooms instead of handing him over to staff. Oh well, if this was how people did things in north Wales, he wasn't going to argue. "Dinner will be at seven, so plenty of time. It's more a supper, really, nothing formal."

"My lady, you needn't trouble yourself, honestly. I'd be more than happy to take a light repast in my rooms."

"We are at cross purposes," the dowager said with a gentle smile, "Although you are more than welcome to attend. This is not a dinner in your honor, although I would be delighted to organize such an event. This is one of our diversions we have every two weeks or so. What with so many people new to the area, on account of the road and bridge planning, it's an entertainment to have ladies and gentlemen attend."

That explained why the driveway to Rosstrevor Hall was so well lit when he'd arrived! "Oh! Thank goodness," he said, as they reached the landing and she guided him towards a suite of room. "I'm really not one for formal dinner parties, you see."

The dowager tilted her head in thought. Then she grinned a little wickedly. "Perhaps that's why there is no countess, and your mother is in such pains?"

"Touché!"

He was beginning to enjoy the company of this playful woman. She and his mother would get along famously.

"Here are your rooms, pull the bell when you're ready and a footman will bring you to dinner, should you wish."

Hannah Jones had been 'at liberty' most of the day as the marquess and his lovely wife had taken to their rooms. With little to occupy her time, she helped the maids as they placed beeswax candles into the polished silver holders.

The dowager marchioness approached with an approving smile and a glint in her eyes. "There you are," she said with a knowing grin. "I take it my daughter-in-law doesn't require you?"

Hannah blushed deeply in confirmation that the marchioness was enjoying private time with her husband. She bobbed a curtsey and said with an air of hope, "Are we lopsided for dinner again?"

The dowager did enjoy creating regular events for the many newcomers to the region. A great many of the men were unmarried, and Lady Mary had taken that as an opportunity.

"You read my mind," the lady handed over a small pot of lotion. "This will remove the smell of the silver polish from your hands."

"Thank you, ma'am," Hannah took the pot and inhaled the lemon scent.

Excitement bubbled within and she followed Lady Mary to her dressing rooms. They were at the opposite wing of the house to where her son resided. A selection of the dowager's dresses were set aside for these occasions. Hannah arrived at Lady Mary's dressing room to find two of the housemaids, Sarah and Anne, already helping each other into borrowed finery.

"Three of us needed tonight?" Sarah said as Hannah and Lady Mary walked in.

"Yes, we have an unexpected guest staying the night, and I have extended an invitation for him to join us. However, he may choose to take his meal in his rooms." She muttered something under her breath about him being a bachelor as she rummaged through her dresses and selected an emerald ensemble. "This will match beautifully with your eyes, Hannah dear."

It was made of layers of translucent fabric, magnificently bunched around the shoulders in matching puffs. The fabric was tighter just under her bust and fell in great drifts of flowing green shades to the floor.

"Now, my dears, let us go through the rules," Lady Mary suggested:

"Smile," Anne said, "and be sweet."

Lady Mary nodded.

Sarah added; "Talk as little as possible."

Another nod from Lady Mary.

Hannah remembered the third rule, "Be polite. They are here to interact with eligible ladies, not staff."

"That's right," Lady Mary said. "And if the topic we do not talk about eventually arises anyway?"

All three said in a chorus, "Tell them the truth, that we have no fortune. When the ladies retire, we may return to our rooms."

Lady Mary clapped her hands. "Excellent!"

Hannah beamed at how well she'd learned this particular set of instructions. "I did hear a whisper that we have an *actual Earl* under the roof tonight."

Anne's brown eyes rounded with surprise. "An earl?"

"Yes," Hannah confirmed.

In a flash, Anne snatched up a silk scarf and wadded it between her chemise and her stays to push her breasts higher.

"You do make me laugh," Hannah said as fixed the puffs on her shoulders.

"Well?" Anne's eye were agog. "Is it true, Lady Mary?"

The lady eventually nodded, and Hannah tried hard not to swoon. "He may not have much fortune himself, he arrived on a horse, not a carriage."

Hannah spoke rapidly, "I wonder if his carriage didn't fall to bits on the road, in which case he might be stuck here for several nights!"

Sarah and Anne squealed in excitement, then Anne reached for a second scarf and began stuffing it into her stays.

"Now, now," Lady Mary rubbed her temple, as if to ward off potential pain. "Very best behavior, please, girls."

Sarah tied the laces at Hanna's back and then patted her shoulder. "All done. Would you mind fixing my hair? You're so good at it."

"Of course!"

The three primped and preened a little longer until Lady Mary clicked her tongue and directed them to the receiving room, where they sat quietly as the guests for the evening arrived.

The dowager's instructions echoed in Hannah's head:

Smile, be sweet, talk as little as possible. You are here to balance out the sexes at the dinner table. They are here to interact with eligible ladies, not staff. If they make a mistake and engage in conversation, be polite. If the topic arises, tell them the truth, that you have no fortune. Later, when the ladies retire, you may return to your rooms.

This would be Hannah's fourth dinner. She'd been exceptionally sweet and smiled at the gentlemen and other ladies at each of the previous three. None of the gentlemen had initiated conversations of any great import with her. The eligible ladies who had come for dinner had more or less ignored her. Hannah had taken no offence at all, as her role on these evenings was to be more or less invisible.

She believed tonight would be no different.

Or at least, it should have been no different, until the most handsome man she'd ever seen stepped into the room and stole the very air from her lungs.

You're going to love the rest of this romance. Click Here to buy it or read on KU.

Author's Note

The Cape Colony, as it was called then, is modern-day South Africa. The British referred to springboks as 'springbucks' in the early 1800s. Springboks are antelope members of the gazelle family. They are known for 'pronking' and springing into the air in acrobatic displays to attract a mate. They can leap more than three meters (10 feet) straight up!

The males and females are known as rams and ewes, and their babies are called lambs. The ewes gestate for around 25 weeks and usually have only one lamb, but if conditions are good they can have two pregnancies a year.

Springboks have adapted so perfectly to their dry and often hot climate, they rarely need to drink. They poor creatures would have been very cold in north Wales!

Crempogs may have a few of you scratching your heads. They are delicious, small fluffy pancakes which are perfect for any time of the day. (In some parts of the world they're known as pikelets)

Ingredients

- 450 ml buttermilk (15 ounces)
- 4 tablespoons or 55 grams (2 ounces) butter
- 275 grams (10 ounces) plain (or all-purpose) flour
- 75 grams (3 ounces) castor sugar (fine sugar)
- 1 teaspoon baking soda
- 1/2 teaspoon salt
- 1 tablespoon vinegar (the baking soda and vinegar help to make the crampons rise)
- 2 large eggs, beaten

You can put everything in together and mix it all up until it's smooth. Then rest for 30 minutes or an hour if you can resist.

Or you can do it the fussy way for crempog perfection.

1. Stir the buttermilk and butter into a saucepan on a low heat and melt them together.

2. Pour the flour into a large bowl and then slowly tip the warmed buttermilk and butter into it. Whisk the batter to remove lumps. Let stand for 30 minutes.

3. In another bowl, beat the eggs and stir in the baking soda, salt and vinegar. Then pour this egg mix into the flour batter and mix well.

4. Oil a heavy fry pan or griddle and get it nice and hot

5. Use a tablespoon to plonk the crempog batter into the pan, in small batches. Cook for a few minutes then turn them over

6. Eat as soon as you like. You can keep them warm by stacking them on top of each other on a plate and covering with a tea towel, in order to serve them all at the same time.

7. Serve with jam or syrup and more butter. Nom!

ALSO BY EBONY OATEN

New Series - Runaway Christmas Brides

My True Love Fled With Me

Available August 26, 2026

Unsuitable Suitors (Sweet Regency)

1. The Christmas Marquess
2. Miss Remington's Steely (Christmas) Resolve
3. Marriage, She Wrote
4. All Roads Lead To Earls
5. Fetch The Christmas Earl
6. A Swain For Miss Penhurst
7. Her Christmas Temptation

Regency Romps (Sexy Regency)

1. There's Something About Miss Mary
2. Hot August Night
3. Scandalous Charlotte
4. Weekend At Baron E's
5. Duke Around and Find Out
6. Romancing The Stone-Cold Rogue
7. Risqué Business
8. Bad News Bonklesford
9. Coming Up In The World

www.ebonyoaten.com

THE BOOKSHOP BELLES

NOVELS CO-WRITTEN WITH CATHERINE BILSON:

Estelle's Ardent Admirer

Marie's Merry Gentleman

Louise's Christmas Champion

Bernadette's Dashing Doctor

THE BOOKSHOP BELLES

In the bustling market town of Hatfield, the four Baxter sisters are doing their best to manage Baxter's Fine Books while their father is away on a book-buying expedition in France. Each sister has her own strengths and dreams, but keeping the bookshop afloat will require all their combined wit, determination, and courage.

From fiery debates to slow-burn romance, the sisters find themselves tangled in unexpected love stories that challenge their beliefs and test their hearts.

• **Estelle**, the practical eldest, clashes with a charming gentleman who upends her carefully ordered life.

• **Marie**, the steady and sensible sister, is stranded in a snowbound castle with a brooding earl and his mischievous sons.

• **Louise**, the no-nonsense protector of the family, finds herself drawn to a towering former soldier with secrets of his own.

• **Bernadette**, the compassionate healer, must learn to work with a dashing doctor whose modern methods challenge everything she holds dear.

Set against the backdrop of a cosy bookshop and a charming Regency town, *The Bookshop Belles* is a heartwarming series about love, family, and the courage it takes to follow your heart.

Perfect for fans of sweet historical romance, these witty, slow-burn love stories feature strong heroines, dashing heroes, and happy endings without on-page sexual content.

About Ebony Oaten

Ebony Oaten loves history, but doesn't like living through it.

She is especially glad she was not around during the Regency era, as she would most likely have died in infancy from asthma, or something hideous like diphtheria. In the unlikely event that she'd made it to adulthood, she would have probably been a scullery maid or a lowly servant, as she 'talked too much and didn't pay attention' because ADHD diagnoses hadn't been invented.

Grab a free, sweet Regency romance novella and join her reading community here.

Or, if you like spicier reads, grab a free, steamy Regency romance novella and join her reading community here.

(You can grab both, and she'll delete email double-ups, it's all good.)

You'll find her website, full of Regency romance catnip, at www.ebonyoaten.com

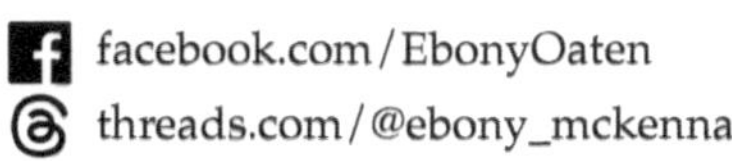

facebook.com / EbonyOaten

threads.com / @ebony_mckenna